For Sarah

You are a great person. Thank you for your encouragement. Here's to a great future for you and for me, whatever we do!

Your friend,
Adam Koupnia
7/18/18

Max's Modern-Day Philosophy

A Novel by Adam Kovynia

Dedication

To my fifth grade English teacher Mrs. Willis. So many years ago, I began to feel encouraged to pursue writing one day because of the great assignments and teaching.

Chapter 1

Another Night

Glancing one last time at the stove, I read the clock. A fluorescent green 10:16 PM glowed in the dim room. I was just about ready to go. My little apartment was cozy and at the end of a dark road, shaded by many trees near a small pond. The apartment itself was a tiny building really. I was the sole inhabitant. The landlords lived next door in a 1920's three family home, renting out a couple floors to tenants. I'd gotten somewhat lucky with the eclectic structure all to myself. One side of the building is rounded, made from stucco painted white while the other side is completely different with a sharp edge and made from bricks. The roof was green and gave off a fairy tale like appearance, so I've been told. Imagine a Thomas Kinkade painting, but not one of those stately mansions. Instead, a tiny cottage near a dirt road. Who was I kidding? My place was too eerie or sinister looking to be in one of his paintings. OK, sinister is a strong word but what else could I afford? Nevertheless, it sufficed, at least for now. It wasn't small-town Connecticut; it wasn't big-city either. Just medium-sized town Connecticut, as far as I saw it anyways. My little corner of the town gave the feel of something much more natural and earthy as compared to downtown anyways. I made the place my own by purchasing this beautiful wooden bookshelf, handmade by a local carpenter, sold at the town flea market, right down the road from me. The shelf rested along one end of the room and my soft, comfy armchair in the corner right next to it. There I'd sit and read so often. It was my little sanctuary. My thoughts snapped back to reality now as I was rushing to get ready for work on time. The aroma of a richly scented medium roast coffee filled the room. Hints of vanilla and chocolate were subtle in the air. I shut off the coffee maker and poured the rest into my travel mug. Holding the coffee in my left hand, keys in my right, and my laptop computer over my right shoulder, I glanced around the room. Pausing to take a few more sips of an ice-cold seltzer, the carbonation pulsed through my veins giving me a boost of energy. I locked the door then swung it shut behind me.

It's another night, typical, but who's to say what will go down at the hotel. Lately, all I can do is hope and pray for a smooth shift at work. Last night was brutal but mostly only for one reason. We'll get to that later.

I didn't plan on working at the hotel for so long. Prior to the hotel, I was on staff full-time at a private academy teaching philosophy here in Connecticut. It was quite an experience and I was proud of it, but it came to an end after one year. They didn't need me anymore; I'm still not quite sure why. But here I was making ends meet on the night shift at a hotel, a job I scrambled to find when I really needed it. I didn't have any commitments holding me down. I was dating Julia seriously while I taught at the academy, but our relationship ended two weeks after I was laid off. Life at the academy was ideal, harmonious, and serene but now things were just kind of humdrum. My life was all routine these days and the stress, although evident from the beginning of my time working at the hotel, was building up now and taking a toll. One year faded into the next and before I knew it I was on my fifth year. Lately I keep thinking: I need a change.

As I step in my car, it's just warm enough that I don't need to let it run for more than a minute. Spring is finally here. It's mid-April and I'm loving this weather. It sure beats two and a half feet of snow! And you know, hotels are open 24/7, 365 days a year-not always easy getting to work in a blizzard. Sure, you can stay in the hotel for free if the weather is bad but then you must pack a ton of stuff: food (you don't have a stove to cook with), PJ's, an extra set of work clothes, boots, shovel, dental floss, the list goes on. But there's something about spring that just spontaneously brings me back to old times. Memories of being a teenager, first year or two having a driver's license, shooting pool at Pine Valley Billiards, my first kiss or just random memories of more recent years that stick for some reason.

I've grown accustomed to driving the backroads now to the extent that it's become a habit. I just can't take the highway anymore with the aggressive drivers. Well, unless I'm running ten minutes late or more, then the highway will get me to work on time. I'm often thinking: do the speed demons really need to be getting to wherever they're heading at a lightning fast pace? Where's the fire?! This dog eat dog, get out of my way mentality seems to be that of most Connecticut drivers.

Sipping coffee is always a pleasure for me and a necessity when I'm getting up in the dark of night still in zombie mode for at least the first half hour or longer-sometimes much longer! Lately I've revisited my collection of eighties music by putting only CDs from this decade in my case. But I have the taste for something different tonight. I never realized how prolific the band "Jars of Clay" were until I started collecting each album they made. To me, they are the Dave Matthews Band of the Christian rock movement. Arguably the top act of all time in the Christian genre of music. They took the clever name "Jars of Clay" from a verse in the Bible in the book of Corinthians which goes something like this: "We have this treasure in jars of clay, to show that this surpassing power belongs to God and not to us." Maybe it's just something about me but I like going back a couple decades and re-living another time through music or movies. Well at least the eighties and nineties make me happy.

As I turn the corner, I slowly enter Beckridge Road, enjoying the colonial homes. Candles are always glowing in each window of this one ancient looking house which sits up on a small hill. The early American homes here contribute to a piece of Connecticut history and charm seemingly preserved forever. An amber colored light at the entrance to a Tudor home on my right always gives me a sense of peace. I'll take whatever I can get. Going by the tavern I always tell myself I'd go drinking to one night, I use its presence as a form of inspiration for the future. It's not like it used to be; friends move down south or out west, and you lose touch with people, especially if you're on the graveyard shift. We do it to ourselves. I've come to realize that. Getting unstuck is a part of life many people must face. We all do it in our own way. Although it seems some people never get stuck. They just keep moving forward with a flow of the perfect American man, however, something tells me that image is created by the media and people just try to live it. It's kind of like art imitating life and life imitating art which in this case is the trap of everyone acting and looking the same. "Normal."

I clock in and I'm ready to work. Yesterday was rough as I mentioned earlier. So, what was so rough about it? We were overbooked. Why? I don't know. Often you never really know. So much goes on during the day in a hotel that you're not there to see. Luckily, you're in bed sleeping and regaining your strength while your co-workers are handling the onslaught of fifty to one hundred plus arrivals on a busy day. You can only come so close to being perfect with your preparations. Perfection doesn't exist after all. Someone is not going to get a top floor room even though it's their preference. Someone else won't get a room far enough away from the pool, elevator, exit door or whatever else they want to be away from or close to for that matter. Here's one:

room close to the exercise room. But if they want exercise, why can't they be OK with a room across the way? They'd burn a few more calories walking there in the first place? How about parking? Let's save that topic for another day when I can break out a hotel map. But let's say the guest does get exactly what they want. Who's to say it won't smell like smoke? Or who's to say it won't be completely fresh, but *to them* it will smell like smoke, or something funny? In their imagination I suppose. But do you have time to investigate the so-called odor? The answer is no. At the hotel, it's: go, go, go or at times: slow, slow, slow depending on whatever comes your way. You've got to be able to handle it all at the drop of a hat. So, cut to the chase, being an overbooked hotel, in last night's case, meant five arrivals due to show with guaranteed reservations held by their credit cards, yet only four rooms available for me to use. You don't need a degree in advanced math to figure that one out. Sending a guest across town to a comparable hotel for **free** because we could not honor their reservation, generally is not something they want considering they are not paying for the room themselves if they are on business here visiting a company they work for or are connected to in some way. But I've got no more time to rehash that night in my mind because I can tell already while I'm up front and center that I've got a gentleman walking towards me ready to ask a question...

Chapter 2

Tough Night at Work

"Hi, can I help you?"

"I'm looking to pick up my dry cleaning. I had a suit; it's a Brooks Brothers. I left it this morning and was told it was same day service."

"Yes, we work with a cleaner that offers same day service. Let me check in the back. Your name please?"

"Alex Hoffman."

"One moment," I said.

I looked all around the small back office area, shuffling through the lost and found nook and in every corner and on every countertop. No sign of the suit was around. Hmmmm…

"Maybe it's been delivered to your room sir? Sometimes they do it that way, but I typically am not here at that time because I'm only working nights, from eleven p.m. till seven a.m.," I said.

"OK, let me run up and check. We just got back from the steakhouse for dinner and I haven't been up in the room for hours," he said.

"In the meanwhile, I'll check around for some notes in case my staff left me any info regarding your dry cleaning also," I said.

I was feeling thirsty, so I walked over to our convenience store section which was conveniently located about fifteen feet away from me. I grabbed a spring water out of the large fridge which was only half stocked and then glanced into the small freezer next to it and saw all the frozen dinners were scattered about. I opened the freezer to organize the mess and felt the dinners were not frozen at all. Next, I reached for a container of ice cream to test its firmness and as I pressed it, I felt a mushiness to it, which is not common since our ice cream is so ridiculously frozen that you need about twenty minutes for it to thaw just enough to stab it with a spoon. This is not good. Clearly the freezer has stopped working, *again*. I checked to see if it was on and so forth, but I knew that since this was a recurring issue I'd have to just move the contents out to the large freezers in the kitchen. I quickly started doing so as not to waste any money on all this food. My radio was dead, so I couldn't speak to my houseman. I plugged it in to charge the battery.

This is frustrating. I'm thinking why does this stuff happen? What did I do to deserve it? I continued to transport the food to the back as quickly as I could. Maybe it could be saved or maybe not. It was still cold and thawing out.

When I returned to the lobby I saw the same businessman from before, only about fifty percent angrier looking.

"Where did you go? I expect someone to be here helping me and I don't appreciate waiting especially when it's late and I need my suit," he said in an uptight tone of voice.

"I'm sorry sir. The freezer stopped working and I just wanted to quickly…."

"It doesn't matter. Where is my suit?" he raised his voice accentuating the word suit.

"I don't see anything sir. Maybe I can call Jill; she was working earlier, she might know something…."

He interrupts me, and I can tell he's very mad. "You know I'm tired and I was working all day. I need that suit for the morning. I've got meetings and I need to be up in a few hours."

Piecing things together in my mind, I really wonder what has happened to this man's suit. I retrieve Jill's number from the computer at a rapid pace and pick up the phone to begin dialing. Calling her is probably going to be of little help but somehow if I keep her on the line long enough it will feel like a lifeline for me because at least it will be *some* support and someone in my corner helping me fight the battle. Every night I have no support… being here all on my own, except for my houseperson, otherwise called a houseman, who cleans and delivers things to the rooms. In addition to that he acts as "security," patrolling the area a couple times per night. Jill is still on the line and we are trying to figure out what to do. Then, finally, Thank God, a break!

"Max, I know what you can do! Call Jim's room! He's staying in the hotel tonight. He was working on testing the TV signals in the rooms after some irate guests complained the game was not coming in. He's got to be up early to cover as manager in the morning. You know he lives so far away so he just decided to sleep here," Jill said, her voice was nasally as usual. I find Jill attractive; she has a boyfriend, so I never would ask her out. I like her sandy-blonde, straight hair and greenish eyes. She has a pointy chin and a slender physique. Sometimes she wears glasses and sometimes not. She's very sweet. Jill's just someone who looked good to me and I got along with at work. Come to think of it, I've been attracted to most women I've worked with but not all. I never crossed the line and flirted inappropriately, although I've seen other guys do it a couple times in my life. With her I got the signal she probably found me attractive because she'd make physical contact by touching me on my side or back. I liked it. I can't speak for everyone but getting attention from women has always been a good thing for me, nothing to complain about thus far in my life anyways. What can I say? I'm probably just wired to have a stronger than average attraction to women but it's a matter of how you live your life morally that counts.

"Jill, you're a life saver! Thank you! I say to her quietly enough not to anger the guest any further. I can feel how perturbed he is from where I'm standing, and a strong sense of impatience is coming off him like a force of negative energy.

I hang up with Jill and quickly explain to Mr. Hoffman that my assistant manager is staying in the hotel and he can be of assistance hopefully. One advantage of not being in management is that you can lean on them for authority or guidance in dire situations, but nevertheless, most of the time being on your own with the graveyard shift, otherwise known as the "night audit" expects out of you: management skills and responsibilities. Of course, the problem is, you're not the owner or general manager of the hotel, so even if you have perfectly reasonable solutions to problems, you get that looming ominous feeling floating over you like a dark cloud which is: you're damned if you do, damned if you don't. I sort of think that management is in the same position, because they are not in total control, since they have a boss and their boss has a boss, and so on and so forth. Perhaps I just care too much, and I am sensitive to these issues. Either way I still think running your own business is better than working under the big corporate CEO. Even a guest at our hotel years ago said it this way: "Work for yourself, that's what God intended." He wasn't saying it directly to me, but I overheard it.

Fast forward ten minutes. I had already called my manager who is staying in house and he agreed to come down to help. There's a back and forth between Mr. Hoffman and my manager Jim, who is dressed in a pair of jeans, pajama top, and slippers. Jim looks more groggy and tired than I do. I've been here for long enough to be wide awake by now. Coffee is steadily coursing through my veins and my heart rate is going faster than normal. But what else is new? Little resolve to this problem is apparent until Jim has a major light bulb moment. "Patti," he says just slightly above a whisper. Patti is our coworker who was on in the morning and stayed late today. She processed the charges for the dry cleaning.

"I'd like to explain this to you sir, straight forward. It's late and I believe I know what has happened to your dry cleaning. Our associate working earlier today went ahead and charged you for the dry cleaning because we can see the charges have posted to your bill on our computer screen in front of me, so I am certain they have been cleaned and returned. It's clearly not in your room as you've told us. We don't see the suit here either, and we looked very carefully I can assure you. In fact, we even checked in all our offices back here. But we had another guest who had dry cleaning delivered to her room today and the only reasonable explanation is that your suit got tangled together with her clothes and ended up in her room. In the morning as soon as we can, we'll be happy to retrieve the suit for you," Jim politely explained to him.

Because it was too late in the night to call the guest with the mistaken dry cleaning, Jim had offered the guest a number of freebies for his dilemma: Free breakfast? No! Free Coffee? No! Free water and snacks? No! A rebate on his room bill? No! And on it went like this.

"Sir we just cannot call at this late hour," Jim continued to explain.

The reality is also that the lady with the mixed up dry cleaning was highly ranked in our membership program which means we must kiss up to her, and especially not wake her up in the middle of the night! Plus, she is a total bitch and we all know it. We have plenty of examples to prove it and she's the last person we want to piss off right now. Unfortunately, Mr. Hoffman is a total jerk and red hot angry at this point.

"Did you know my TV signal was hardly coming in at all yesterday?" Then he turned and looked at me with anger in his eyes. "Why don't you do something and take action instead of just standing over there??!!" he yelled at me while I stood back a few feet away from them and listened intently.

I didn't answer him because there was nothing more that I could do at that point. All the answers were given, and he just wasn't accepting it.

My manager had another option up his sleeve. "We'd like to give you two hundred dollars out of our drawer so that you can purchase a suit if you'd like. There is a 24-hour shopping center we can provide you with directions for which should be able to accommodate what you're looking for. We know that it's......"

The guest refused the money and continued to put up an argument also threatening to dial customer service to complain about both of us, yet he kept ending the call as he got about halfway through dialing. This continued for several more minutes until finally Mr. Hoffman accepted the situation at hand and went to bed.

I was back on my own and suddenly got two phone calls coming in at about the same time. Did I mention the obnoxious sound of our phone system? It's enough to give you a panic attack if not a heart attack and designed to get you to pick it up quick. You don't want to hear it ring another time.

"Yeah, my toilet is not flushing," a guest said with a somewhat rude, somewhat uncivilized tone of voice.

"I'm going to send someone up right away; I'm sorry about that."

I went to reach for my walkie talkie. I pressed down the button to speak and I got no response from my houseperson. Hmmm, the battery is good by now I'd think. I tried again. And again. Dammit, I thought to myself. Lightly I slammed my fist down on the counter. I didn't want to stoop to the level of our more volatile guests, so I kept my patience, *barely*. I started running down the hallway to look for my houseperson. I came to the end and turned back. I went down the other hallway to check if he was mopping the pool area. No luck. I checked in the breakroom. Nothing. Then in the employee restroom. It was locked. I called after him and he explained he's in the bathroom and he'd be out soon. I let him know which room to attend to as soon as he could.

I remembered the other phone line was ringing but I couldn't get to it. By the time I returned to the lobby I heard the phone ringing nonstop. I raced for it and handled the guest's request for a wake-up call. I could set the wake-up calls so fast now that I'd practically be able to do it blindfolded in a matter of 2 seconds. But setting wake up calls, stocking sodas and candy bars was easy. Counting cash, printing reports were all the simple, pleasant aspects to the job as well. My night didn't get much better. I'd had more complaints for completely unrelated reasons and the pressure was killing me, not to mention my leg started to hurt and the floor was hard, no wonder. This job was not the perfect image of health.

Everything had come to a head at this point. In fact, beyond the problems of nights like this, sleeping in the daytime had become, for the past year especially, more and more difficult. The absurdity of making myself sleep while it was perfectly bright and sunny out in the middle of the day was just plain crazy. Today, after work in the morning I'd speak to my manager and let him know I needed a break. He'd been there with me for at least half an hour last night to see the kind of BS that I deal with. Of course, he was free to go back to bed afterwards and I had to stay up to finish my shift.

Chapter 3

It's All Just Complaining?

I got home in the morning and still did not know what to do, so I figured calling an old friend might be right. I just could not get myself to speak to management right away. I needed a job after all, especially for health insurance coverage and didn't want to rush into making the wrong decision. Could I take a break for longer than the typical one or two-week vacation and still return to a job? Speaking of vacation, I was on vacation last summer in

Maine-first time there-the town of Kennebunkport, heard all great things about it and said, why not, I'll make the drive up. Great art galleries, great atmosphere. So, I was there outside having a coffee with a view of the ocean. This guy struck up a conversation with me. He was most definitely an extrovert. Coincidentally he also worked at a hotel. He was there with his girlfriend, but I didn't see her, she was off looking at jewelry nearby. He sat down, and we had a conversation about the hotel business and somehow ended up laughing about an episode of Seinfeld. I believe it was with Jerry getting arrested in a parking garage. I didn't have a place to stay because I was really playing my spontaneous trip by ear. He convinced me to stay at his hotel. I suppose I got a lesson in hotel sales by the end of our conversation just through osmosis. He'd have the night off so later he'd come by and have a drink with me and another member of the staff there. His girlfriend came along also. The guy's not online anywhere, that I can find him anyways. But he said, "Give me a call anytime," along with a firm handshake, "we'll chat, talk hotel stuff," he said. Me, I'm an introvert and I just thought this guy is cool in a way that I can respect. It wouldn't hurt to have a contact like that. Maybe good on a resume as a reference at the least.

So, I call him up. After all, he said, "call me anytime." Now is the time that I would need to call him. Shoot the breeze, ask for his advice. I've never been in such a fork in the road before. It wasn't like me to call someone like this out of the blue, but I'd done all kinds of things back in college. Lake Ontario Beach University, in New York state, where I'd gotten my bachelor's degree in philosophy, was a place where I'd felt comfortable having many conversations with many different people. I'd taken a "learn from everyone" approach and written countless pages of essays based on what I've learned. Now who better to turn to than this guy Ryan from Maine who'd reached out to me and conversed with me for an extended period. Upon my leaving he said to me, "The ball's in your court," meaning it'd be up to me to call and re-connect. So, I pick up the phone and dial him.

"Max, what's up buddy. Are you interested in buying any antiques?"

"No, no sorry, I'm just kind of stressed, I figured I'd call you because you said, 'call anytime.'"

"You coming up to Maine again? You can stop by my place. Beth and I are engaged now," Ryan said.

"Really? Congratulations."

"Thanks, so what's up dude?"

"Well, you still work at a hotel? I asked.

"No, quit a couple months ago," he said.

"I had the worst night of my life," I said.

"What happened? Busy? Mean customers?" he asked.

"Overbooked! and *then some*, well… overbooked earlier in the week, *then* we had issues with, well, all kinds of stuff outside of my control, maintenance, engineering issues and you know there's nobody to deal with that stuff at night… it's just me," I said.

"You've got your houseperson, right?"

"Yeah but they can't really ...

"Yeah, I know they can't fix all that stuff but what you need to do is work *with* the system, go with the flow, don't work against it. When someone is pissed about being bumped from their reservation, you need to tell them we had rooms being put out of order to fix the tubs or better yet talk about fixing the smoke detectors, carpets being washed…" he said.

"Yeah, yeah, but I don't lie to people," I said, accentuating the word lie.

"You've got to get to the solution and stop getting stuck on the problem dude. If you keep…" Ryan said.

"I know what you're saying," I cut into his sentence.

"No, you are just not making things work for you…"

"I feel that it's all about greed when you really get down to it because if they never overbooked those rooms to begin with then…" I started to explain.

"You're complaining; stop complaining. Wake up and smell the coffee Max… you drink coffee, right?" Ryan said, with a hint of sarcasm in his voice.

"I drink coffee. Trust me, I drink coffee, but I have a reason to complain. Do you realize what this guy said to me yester..."

"Hey man, I'm sorry but I've got to go. Beth's calling me from the other room. Hang in there dude. Take care man! Keep in touch!" he said.

As I heard the phone click, I wondered- is it all just complaining? *Why* do other co-workers of mine not vent a whole lot to me? Do they lie when they act happy? Do they keep it within by bottling up their emotions most of the time? Do they just come and go without sticking it out?... I can't just leave… I need money. I know my conversation with Ryan isn't going to solve anything. I'm up to my eyeballs with stress and I need a solution...

Chapter 4

I've Had Enough

I called Jim. "Listen Jim, I had the

toughest week of my life at work. You were
there that night with the dry-cleaning guy; he
was furious, remember? And the overbooked
hotel rooms before that and all that went wrong.
I need a break; I've got two weeks of paid time
off at least but I don't think I can make it
through next week let alone tonight. I looked
ahead at the computer and we are overbooked
by five rooms next Monday plus overbooked by
seven on Tuesday. I don't know what's going
on, but the pressure is too much. I need to take a
leave of absence or something, but I've never

done that before. I haven't slept enough, and nights are killing me."

"Wait, wait a minute Max, I know you've worked here forever. You've talked before about how you sleep so well. You're hardly ever sick, maybe *never* sick. You don't call out. You drive here in a snowstorm. You're very dedicated," he said.

"Well I do, I am, I mean the sleep thing has just changed for me in the past year I think. How do I explain it? It's just like I've gotten a little older and my life is changing. I have a few more aches and pains plus maybe my body is just rejecting the backwards sleep cycle finally. They're cutting trees down in my neighborhood lately which makes falling asleep a challenge and the overbooked rooms are a major source of tension for me. It's like, no matter how I go over it in my mind, it's always stressing me out," I said.

"Don't let it ruin your day, we are all on the same team," he said.

"But is there a way I can just take a break?"

"Uhhmm, well.... your shift is hard to fill… Max, give me one hour. I'm going to give you an answer, because you deserve one," he said.

I walked over to my big, comfy armchair. Put my phone down on the coffee table and picked up a book. I glanced over modern architecture of Hong Kong and got up after a few minutes to make myself a double sized mug of hot organic green tea with honey. For a while I took a little mental vacation to Asia. I took a deep breath and tried to remind myself that I was in control of my life ultimately and things would work out. I had started regular prayer recently, always including the Our Father or Lord's Prayer. I spoke to God, asking him for certain changes in my life. Sometimes I got specific and sometimes I was general. But I knew that I had a lot to learn because the difference between my new age philosophies and my Christian faith were at odds in some ways. I tried to wrap my mind around such a simple concept as "God is in control", as written by Charles Stanley, a guy I saw preaching on television late one night. He certainly spoke with great confidence. It felt like a paradox to me, but I wanted it to be true: God is in control.

The phone rang, and Jim wasted no time. "Listen Max, Marcus from our other property can cover because he's looking for more hours and I can pick up most of the rest. We'll figure out the remainder of shifts from week to week. I don't know… I just feel maybe if this is what you need then you deserve it. I've never heard you like this before. You're obviously feeling beaten up, spent. We're giving you a month, starting today. Look, it's Thursday morning. Typically, you work Thursday night and you have Friday and Saturday nights off. So, stay home tonight, don't do anything I wouldn't do, and don't come back until the 15th of next month. That gives you a month entirely. Enjoy Max, we appreciate what you're doing," he said, with a smile in his voice and a chuckle.

"Listen Jim, thank you, thank you, I really mean it." And with that, I knew this would be my time.

The reality began to sink in. I had some decent time to myself. I had to decompress sort of like the way I would just sit in my car after a tough shift at work. Sometimes for as long as twenty minutes. Once I finished my tea, I took a long walk outside. The hour I spent out in nature got my blood flowing once again. I said a thank you prayer to God and looked forward to a good night's rest. I'd been up all night and it was now late morning. I'd just stay up for as long as I wanted, then crash in my bed later. For now, I'd fix myself a cup of coffee. In fact, I'd drink as many coffees as I'd want today.

Sitting down at my desk, I took a slow deep breath and opened the drawer and took out my notes. I'd been working on a journal of philosophical essays I'd put into a book, one day.... I know it's silly but it all kind of began when I was on a vacation in Florida one year as a kid. I was only ten years old and my family plus some extended family were all there. But for some reason I was just alone at that moment walking along the shore in sunny Cocoa Beach, Florida. I guess I was always imaginative but now as my thoughts started forming, I asked myself different questions about life and one led to another. It wasn't the typical adult-like worrying where the questions just keep coming leaving you feeling depressed. Oh no, this was different. In fact, it was not depressing at all. It was a happy moment. I felt alive intellectually as I realized that I was like a little philosopher and it was pretty cool. So as time went on I decided to pursue it on the college level. Some joked about Lake Ontario Beach University, but others respected it. Sure, it didn't have the gothic, picturesque structures of Nazareth College, where I'd attended a talk about the Vatican once. Or maybe it didn't have the reputation of University of Rochester or nearby RIT, however, it had a cool modern looking building or two plus a simple massive wing to hold the rest of classes. The dorms and apartments overlooking the lake were memorable for me. Sometimes I even got a little sad thinking about it. All of us, pretty much scattered after graduation. The good times lived on in my memories at least.

I leafed through my notebook and came across this page:

Medjugorje: a small mountain village in south eastern Europe. Located in Bosnia and Herzegovina, part of the former Yugoslavia. In 1981 six young people, a combination of boys and girls had visions and communication with

Mother Mary. Since then many thousands of people have traveled to the holy site and experienced hundreds of healings. Cured of Cancer, drug addiction, multiple sclerosis. *note* research more, look at book from Bloomfield Library and watch Unsolved Mysteries, continue to compile information…

I read my notes on Medjugorje and sat back in wonder. I still had more research to do it seemed, but I had accumulated at least two pages of writing. I continued to flip through my essays and stopped on a page which read:

Essay Ideas:

- "What would a Ron Paul Presidency Look Like?"
- "What are the Arguments for and Against Having a Pope?"
- "How Many Lives Does a Vegetarian Save Per Year?"
- "Political Correctness in Our American Society"
- "Public Schools VS. Private Schools"
- "Why Christian Rock Music is Not what It Used to Be"
- "What Exactly is Post Modernism?

- "Christian films, Mainstream films: Is a Middle Ground Possible?"

I stopped to think about a Ron Paul presidency. That was an old essay I'd written but always found someone at a party somewhere willing to argue with me about it. Funny thing I realized one day was that I reached a point where I didn't get too worked up over it all anymore. I sort of knew I was right in many of my points in defending a Ron Paul limited government philosophy and was comfortable with agreeing to disagree with anyone on politics. The thing I realized though was that I'd talk, talk, talk, and later in the night I'd found the person I was debating with felt kind of beaten up by the whole thing, meanwhile I was elated by the experience. So, I started to become more aware of my level of kindness or maybe lack there of when getting into politics. Several other big names came about since Ron Paul in the world of conservative republican, tea partiers, or libertarians, yet I began losing interest in focusing my energy on those topics. I'd also felt humbled by my lack of knowledge when I started to realize how complicated healthcare, the gun debate and economics were. It's not that I changed my political viewpoint but just that I knew I had a lot more to learn.

I suddenly came up with a new topic for an essay. **"The Upside of My Hotel Experience as a Night Auditor"** This Particular essay wouldn't necessarily end up in any book, but I just feel I need to write out my thoughts. Working at night is a solitary experience for about half the time you're there. When things quiet down you can use your spare time to surf the internet, read a book, magazine, sketch or do any number of things. Although it's not as relaxing as doing it yourself at home, it's still better than nothing. When you have a houseperson to work with that you get along with, it's another bonus. Your house person is your teammate. You need to cooperate. You've got to stay safe. Check your walkie talkies to see if they work. Communicate effectively so that he or she can get what you need done quickly. But you may not talk much to your houseperson because even though you get along fine, he or she might have limited English language abilities or just not a whole lot in common. This sparks my memory of working with Dorothy. She's not a regular houseperson but instead a housekeeper who cleans guest rooms during the day and she's been working for the company for almost thirty years. That's hard to believe because she looks young and she's also very energetic. When I first came on here I noticed this about her and several people always said something to the effect of: "Teach me how to be so happy all the time Dorothy." She's energetic in an eccentric and almost zany kind of way really but that's not an insult. It goes to show each person is different in their own way. The more I think about it, she makes me feel good because I realize that we are all different in our own way. So, the whole reason why I bring her up is because I worked with her on the overnight shift when there was nobody else left to cover. Let's say my regular houseperson was out sick or on vacation for a week. It would be a pleasure to work with Dorothy because our conversations went on forever. She's

American and there's no language barrier here. The night went by quicker, although she didn't have so much time to do her work, yet we had a blast talking non-stop about all things related to our hotel. A little bit of gossip, sure but also plans about my future. I'd talk to her about my dreams. Some of them a little out of left field. Like packing up my car and driving across the country then stopping in a place like Grand Island, Nebraska for instance. If I'd like it there maybe I'd just stay for good.

You realize working in a hotel has some pluses. Even from a Christian perspective, in this industry you are serving others. It can be good or bad and sometimes you really feel it. You feel it saps the energy right out of you but on the other hand it can serve as a way to ask yourself the common question I've been asking myself for the past while: "What Would Jesus Do? AKA WWJD?" Potentially the hotel can offer an opportunity for you to serve others the way Jesus would want you to. Underneath the surface of it all there's a lot of greed, coming from the top. The whole system is really corrupted yet many people don't see it that way. One night a guy walked into our building after being sent away by our competitors across the street. He'd been pretty upset and although it's easy for us to deal with his frustration because it's not directed at us but at the hotel across the street, it's still ridiculous to see this man so upset and not realize the same thing happens at our hotel. My co-worker was there and happened to deal with the man, which she did beautifully by setting him up with a room at our place. Although she was a ten on the fakeness scale, she got the job done. In my case, I stood back in the distance and wondered why more people didn't realize the problems they face at the competitors are just the same problems they'd face with us eventually. Also, the main frustration is that the man or woman behind the counter most likely is not responsible for the overbooking of a hotel room. That happens for numerous reasons. The likelihood of the whole system changing is about the same as the odds that someone like Ron Paul would have actually been voted into the office of Presidency in the United States. Wasn't this essay supposed to be about the good? Well, this much I realized: if you picture a scale in your mind and you weigh the good and the bad on either side, the bad outweighs the good but I'll explain why. Call it the pros and cons, whatever you'd like. You can place all the pros on one side and list quite a few such as: a generous discount for yourself, family and friends, the opportunity to move up career wise, a clean environment, well clean enough etc., but on the other hand the negatives might or might not total the same amount as the positives yet just one brutal negative can feel like ten tons crushing your spirit. Now back to Dorothy my co-worker, conversations with her will always be remembered long after I leave the job. Talking with her could be the encouragement I need to pursue publishing another work in philosophy like these essays I'm leafing over now. And you don't always get that encouragement from your family now or growing up for that matter. They may have expected you to do something different with your life or not known at all how to really be parents in all the right ways. Reaching out and making connections and friendships with co-workers or people out there can be the difference that makes the difference in your life.

I'd have the rest of the day to myself and I had a lot of energy now. I got up to make another cup of coffee, this time adding ground cinnamon to the grind. I turned on my CD player and put in David Sanborn's 'Songs from last night' album. I continued to write more and research more long into the day. I blew out the hazelnut candle I had burning for the past several hours so that I would not fall asleep with it on. After that final cup of coffee, I struggled over to my bed trying to decide whether or not I had the strength to change into my pajamas. I really should I thought. OK so I did, for extra comfort.

Chapter 5

This is My Time

T his   thought kept playing over in my mind: This is my time, this is my time. I had a month and it was not enough time to sleep on it. I had to put it to use but still recharge my batteries.

Cousins are like friends and I've always considered these two cousins like best friends of mine. Bob and Sally, siblings, are about my age; we're all in our 30s. I just get along with them well and feel comfortable around them. We made impromptu plans, and I'm coming to pick them up. I've got a coffee in hand, even though its late, after eight p.m. It's my night off from work and I don't have to think about going back for weeks so I'll enjoy this cup of Green Mountain Coffee Roasters for the ride. It's Nantucket Blend, among my favorites, unsweetened almost always with extra milk, not too strong nor too weak. I'm much more specific about my coffee than about my women. Is that a good thing? It's beautiful out, the wind blowing a warm breeze. It's unseasonably warm for this time in April but no one's complaining. We're all loving it, in fact that's all I heard on Channel 3 today. Driving by a lake I see the shimmering reflection of apartments. The Naked Eyes Greatest Hits CD is playing in my car, a real gem from the 80s. Around the bend, pine trees fill the earth all around this winding road, deer have crossed this area I recall but haven't been out much in the past couple years to my memory. Come to think of it, they've probably been out just the same, but I haven't been. That's what night shift will do to you. You miss out. On my days off, I'm home sleeping at the oddest time of day. I continued to drive, periodically sipping my coffee still hot to the touch. I noticed a mostly full bottle of Poland

Spring water on the back seat. "Bonus!" I gulp down most of the bottle in no time. An ancient cemetery is up on a hill to my left. I love seeing the lights on in people's house's. Surprisingly, you'd think I'd enjoy that a little more going to work, especially taking the backroads but sadly by the time I'm on the road during the week people are off to bed typically and lights are out *and* if they are on and I'm working a Friday or Saturday night on those rare occasions they need me to cover a weekend shift, I just can't enjoy glancing by and looking at the houses because the tension is always a bit higher within me on a Friday or Saturday night going into work. The hotel gets crazy on Fridays and Saturdays. The people who walk through the front lobby entrance are sketchy; some are just plain dangerous. The noise complaints are a challenge which I would not wish on my worst enemy.

I couldn't help but take the backroads this far but ultimately, I'd have to jump on the highway now. Sure, I could go through the bad part of the city, but the roads are going to do a number on my car with all those potholes. Driving through Hartford on the highway requires paying attention and quick thinking. Indeed, I'd have to admit it looked beautiful with all the tall buildings lit up. I think overall my favorite memories from my twenties out in Hartford were on the cobblestone Pratt Street at a club which went out of business many years ago, but I'll never forget it. And who can forget City Steam Brewery on Main street? Where else can you shoot pool with a juke box playing in one room, then go watch live music in the next room while ordering beer made in house, later see a comedy show downstairs? it's one of a kind. One night there I was even asked to dance by a UCONN med student. When I came back after using the bathroom, she was already dancing with another guy. Good times nonetheless.

By the time I get to Manchester I am full of adrenaline from the highway. But I walk over to their aparment and ring the doorbell.

"Hi Max!" Sally said.

"Hi cuz," I responded.

"How's it going Philosophy Max?" she said calling me by a rarely used nickname the two of them bestowed upon me.

"Great, can't complain," I responded.

I stop to think…. I'm not really doing great but I'm an optimist. I've always been one. Maybe it's like Ryan from Maine said on the phone. It's all just complaining?...hmmm, I know I learned this much: not everyone will give you sympathy about your struggles at work. For instance, you tell some people you're tired and wiped out from work; they just giggle and tell you to get more rest. You talk to others and they give you advice but it's not the advice you want to hear. Maybe they play a role, like a family member just looking out for you…. Lost in thought, I completely phased out what my cousin Sal was saying for the past minute.

"Oh, sure I'll have a glass of water," I said.

"Ready to go bud?" Bob called out walking down the stairs. "Let's head out fellas."

We drove past the Main Pub. Live music tonight, the sign read. "We've got to go there one day guys," Sally said.

"Hartford Road Café also, Hungry Tiger too," I added to the conversation.

One-time Alfred Hitchcock said, "Happiness is having nothing to worry about on your plate." That's how I feel now, but again, at the same time, I must do something soon if I want to eliminate what will eventually be on my plate again a month from now.

We passed the Manchester/Vernon town line and kept driving. There was something special about just glancing out the window and living in the moment which I had to relish as I knew good times are not guaranteed to last. Maybe I wasn't such an optimist after all. I blame the hotel! We entered the historic Rockville part of town. I admired the old hospital building and all its regal architectural features. The old mill up ahead on the right reminded me of something out of Transylvania somehow. We continued up a winding road.

"Put it on lite 100.5 at least if you're not going to play your own music Bob. Give me something," I said finally noticing that it was silent in the car.

"Oh, shut up Max."

"Hey, be nice," his sister scolded.

"We're almost there," Bob said meanwhile Sally turned the radio on and adjusted the station and volume. The song "Hold on my Heart" by Genesis was playing. I let out a sigh and felt happy. I also realized this had to be lite 100.5 otherwise it was close enough.

We'd arrived on the lake front bar where the parking lot was rather full. People even parked on the grass. "First round is on me guys", Bob offered.

"OK I'll take that, get me a Leinenkugel's if they have it," I said.

"Leinenkugel's?"

"Yeah Leinenkugel's, you've heard of it? You know, brewery in Chippewa Falls, Wisconsin," I remarked.

"Yeah, yeah, I know, inside joke between us all. How can I forget about that case you brought over? The three of us went through that case quick, r-e-a-l quick. Sunset Kiss I think, no Sunset Wheat," Bob said amused.

"Yeah, if not, get me something different, I'm feeling adventurous."

Bob returns with Sally and I'm sitting there just glancing over at this one woman, thinking to myself. Hmmm... I'm single... doesn't hurt to look. Dark brown hair, curves, nice hips. She got my attention, I don't think I'd ever get tired of looking at her.

"Hey, I saw you looking at her," Bob said.

"Bob, she's cute," I respond.

Bob put down a bucket of Dos Equis, Corona, and Sam Adams. A combo of beers, an assortment on ice. "You want tortilla chips and salsa?" he asked.

"They sell it up there," Sal followed up.

"Sure, thanks," I responded. "You know, this place is cool."

"I told you it was, I had been here before on my own one time and I just thought it was different, not really a restaurant but with a small menu, open about half the year, outdoor seating. Closed in the colder months. Beautiful, trees along the lake, nature and all, people talking, laughing. Something you could be doing more often Max," he said.

"You're a bit of a loner Max. I think that's what my brother here is getting at," she said stopping to take big gulps of beer in between her words.

"I know, but I like it that way."

"Yeah, yeah, Mr. Philosophy Boy," Bob chimed in.

"I'll take that as a compliment cuz."

"You'll twist everything into a compliment Max; you're optimistic. I'll give you that," Bob said.

"But lately it's hard, the hotel gig is building up with pressure and..."

"Well, just get out of there," she responded.

"I know but…." I said while still having my eyes fixated on that woman in the distance.

"Wait, what about that girl you're looking at there, she's not so cute," Bob said.

"I think she's cute, she's gorgeous," I said, taking a swig of my beer.

"She's got that navy-blue polo shirt, right?

"Yeah, her, with dark brown hair, shoulder length, tied back, blue jeans," I explained.

"The jeans are too tight, for her weight," Sally said.

"Everyone wears it like that," Bob added.

"But I'm not sure I agree with you here Max. Why *gorgeous*? You got strange taste," Bob said.

"Well, if I got so called strange taste in women, then so be it," I said.

"You know, she's kind of flat chested," Sal begins to look more closely. "And I don't think she's got a good figure max, but if you...…"

"Well, I'm really turned on by her *and* I like her body, she's hot," I said.

"Max, did you forget to put in your contact lenses tonight? Perhaps it's time to schedule your eye exam. A new RX, OK just kidding, she's just not *my* type, that's all," Bob said.

Bob has been divorced for three years now. He dates, he's more outgoing than me, I'll admit. He has no kids. Neither does Sally. She's never been married. Engaged once to a guy who left her when he said it wasn't feeling right. She's fun, has a great personality, and a good job at an insurance company. She got over the guy who left her, then met a new guy. Got serious with him and moved in together and stayed in the same place for two years until she started getting emotional and rethinking her whole life. Why am I with him? Will he leave me like the last guy? Do I have trust issues? Maybe I don't need a guy right now she thought. So, she left him. Her and her brother split the rent and live together at the place in Manchester until they figure out the next step in their life. Over all, us cousins, aunts, uncles, etc. are all pretty supportive of each other.

Me, I've had a few girlfriends over the years. Sure, the last one left me after I lost my job at the academy. But prior to Julia, there was a real "new ager" whom didn't always see eye to eye with me on things. Ironically, I was big into the new age at the time but still held to many Christian beliefs simultaneously. One day we were at a new age shop. You know the kind which sells incense, crystals, books, candles and does psychic readings and such. She'd said, about a famous author in the new age genre: "He and she split. They were married for a few years." I told her that it was sad. But she said, "Maybe they got everything they needed from each other." I told her that I believe my view of marriage is different from her view of marriage, in the sense that I was old fashioned in how I viewed it. Around that same time, I'd been reading a personal journey/new age type of book written by this lady who went on a life changing quest. Everything was incredibly inspiring for me up until I got to the chapter of the book which dealt with sexuality and freedom of sexual expression. You know, stuff like that. I stopped to ponder where that fit into a Christian worldview. Somehow it just didn't feel pure to me. I wondered if the correct choice for me was to exclusively become a Christian. That was then but as for now since the past couple of months I have been a Christian exclusively.

While I was deep in thought, Sally and Bob talked to each other. Their words were not understandable partly because of the noise rippling through the place and because I was lost in my imagination.

"Hey Philosophy Boy, earth to Max," Bob called out.

I glanced over at Bob for a second then glanced over across the distance to see if she was still there. The girl in the navy-blue polo shirt. I could not believe my luck. We made eye contact, and something just felt right.

I got up and put one hand on Bob's shoulder. "Be back cuz, don't drink all my beer," I said with a smile on my face.

I walked towards her. This was my chance. Before you know it, one week will be over, then two, then three and so on. Seize the day. I might as well use a lesson from that "Dead Poet's Society" movie. Although I don't think that film had much of a happy ending, you catch my drift.

I asked her if she knew what time the place closes, not a bad thing to ask. It came to me spontaneously. I didn't have a plan if you could tell.

"Hmm uh I don't know," she responded.

"Nice here huh, you've been here before? I asked.

At that point, she knew, and I knew what was going on here. Flirting and somehow, I broke the ice so quickly and I was relieved about that.

Again, we caught eyes and were directly looking at each other for a moment. Now I can see that her eyes were a dark brown and I just loved the way she looked as I studied the features of her face. She also happened to be as tall as me which is taller than average for a woman.

We started talking about beer. Easy segue. What are you drinking and what are your favorite drinks. What are the ingredients in a Long Island Iced Tea? Tequila Sunrise is a really tasty drink. What was the original martini? Stuff like that. Next thing you know we are just standing there and talking for probably five minutes. I got the feeling she was impressed by my Connecticut trivia. She was surprised with how much I knew, and she told me so. She's leaning against a wooden beam; her friends are giggling and looking over while sitting at their picnic table. Large candles were glowing on each table and up higher a string of blue and green lights all along the perimeter giving off a mysterious and hazy light. This place was cool when I first arrived, but now it's just plain magical. And I still have not even taken a celebratory shot of liquor with Bob and Sally. Celebratory was just what we called it each time for a joke. What a way to start off my "vacation." Her friend called her over and she had to go, but we exchanged information and I left happy.

My cousins and I did have that celebratory shot of liquor. This time we made it a spiced rum. We chatted over a couple more beers. Bob paced himself and was OK to drive he'd said. We decided to head back home and hopped in the car to drive off.

"What're you doing back there Max? Texting her? Sal asked.

"Yeah, hey you know she went to college at Bob Jones University?

"Really, Bob Jones? wwhhaaat? What kind of school is that? It's like Mike Smith University, funny name no offense, never heard of it," Sal said.

"Well I have. I even had a catalog to that school and I remember looking through it. I was quite drawn to it actually," I responded.

"But what is it like?"

"It's a Christian school, more like very fundamentalist Christian. And it's in South Carolina. It's been run by three generations of the same family. They've all been named Bob Jones. Like Bob Jones Sr., Jr., and the Third. Get it?"

"Oh yeah, one of those," said Bob.

"I think what appeals to me is the fact that they take the Bible so seriously, rather than watering down..." I started to say.

"Hey, since when are you a Bible thumper? Are you a born again Christian Max? I get it...she goes to places like this and dumps unsuspecting guys in the lake as a form of baptism," Bob joked.

We all started laughing. Although I was getting irritated at them on the one hand, I'd also been riding a wave of happiness at this moment and let it be. After all, the last good laugh I had was watching pranks on YouTube. And before that, listening to Bax and O'Brien on their morning radio show. In fact, I can't recall the last time I laughed with another person. Again, blame it on the hotel.

"What's her name again?" Bob asked.

"Kate." I said

"OK, we'll toast to Kate and Max in one minute once we get in the apartment."

We rushed into the apartment and bolted up the stairs. Bob rummaged through the kitchen cabinets. "We've got Midori, the green liquor from Mexico, it's the…"

"I know Midori Bob, we need something stronger perhaps," I said.

"OK, OK, Sake, Gordons Gin, Triple Sec, Absolute Pear Vodka.."

"Yeah, Yeah, the Absolute," I yelled out.

"Your wish is my command," he responded.

We sat around the living room with the TV on a channel that played music continuously. 1990's Favorites were on. Bob came by with three shot glasses and we each raised our hands up high. "I'd like to say a toast," I began to say, "I had a good time tonight and things are starting to come together, I hope. Here's to Friday nights and to Kate; we said we'd toast to her after all! Who's got an opener?"

"I do," Bob took out his keys and popped open all our beers. We enjoyed another couple of rounds. Bob and Sal both let me stay on the couch since I'd been drinking for the past few hours. Pretty soon I drifted off to sleep.

Chapter 6

A Fresh New Morning

Morning arrived, and I got up comfortably, believe it or not. I think mainly because of my positive mood shift. There was a feeling of something special in the air which probably had to do with the fact that not only was it a weekend, but I had a month to explore my life, explore the landscape of places all around me and get some decent sleep. Come to think of it, the weekend, lately while I've been working for the past year or so has seemed melancholy for me. Is it because I knew I'd have to return to work in a day or so, or just something even deeper under the surface of my mind? Sometimes I'd question it when I was dating my ex-girlfriend. We'd be out on a Saturday; although I was grateful to be with her and doing our thing, I'd silently question whether I was spending my time in the wrong way. Or was it just fatigue from a backwards sleeping cycle being turned upside down on my days off? I think it was a combination of all these things.

"Can I have a cup of coffee?" I asked Bob.

"You can have at least a cup, and help yourself to breakfast, if you'd like."

I made a coffee and took a healthy-looking granola bar for the road. A brand I'd never seen before. Gave Bob a fist bump and said goodbye to Sal, headed out the door promising I'd talk to them soon.

It was my time now and I started thinking about my life. Often, I'd get this feeling driving to work about wanting to be free from my job and I'd get enticed by the different places on the road I'd see to my left and right while driving to work. Sure, most of the businesses were closed by 10:30 at night, but some still had the lights on. Maybe the staff was mopping the floors, vacuuming, counting the cash, and locking up in their final procedures of the night. I'd see myself coming back here to this same road when I'd no longer work at the hotel and stop in to these places or just drive aimlessly down some side roads and feel a sense of freedom. Like a new man. I'd be experiencing this road like most everyone else. Regular people, not stuck, enslaved by the graveyard shift. But I was sleeping in the day, missing out on a fun meal in the evening. Hell, I couldn't even see the sunset. I was sound asleep while it was happening most of the time.

So, as these thoughts were swirling around my head, I just kept driving further down the road from where my cousins lived. The old Chuck Berry tune popped into my head. *"Riding along in my automobile…with no particular place to go."* I pulled into a gift shop which I'd seen before but never visited. It was also a florist. I'd get flowers for the new lady I met but not just yet. Plus, I didn't know when I'd see her next. Soon maybe, hopefully. I started looking through the candles, picking up each and smelling them. Fresh Orange. Interesting, I never see that scent. Typically, it's mixed with cinnamon or something else, maybe tangerine or mandarin. But orange alone is nice. Why? because it reminds me of Florida. Something special about the place, not just Disney World, which is my favorite, but all the little gift shops and random attractions. Take orange bubble gum for instance, I got a little box of that as a kid once at a gift shop in Daytona Beach. Weird how those little memories can mean so much, so many years later. I continued looking through the candles. Sandalwood and myrrh had a sacred and holy scent, something I could use to give my apartment a calm feel. I eventually bought a rather large cranberry spice scented candle I'd give to Kate when I'd see her next. I'd wrap it up nice and tie a ribbon on it with a little note card.

So why wait any longer? Carpe diem, seize the day. Let's text Kate now. Why text? Why not call. OK I convinced myself to call.

"Hello this is Kate. Max is that you?"

"Yes, it's me."

"Nice to hear from you."

"It's Saturday and I just figured I'd give you a ring because maybe you had some spare time and maybe you would be interested in getting a coffee this evening, afternoon or whenever."

"I'd like that. I had a really nice time talking with you at the bar on the lake."

"I know we didn't talk long but ..."

"No but it was just right, everything seemed so right," she said.

"I know, and that doesn't happen often to me, I have to admit, so I'm glad we met, and I decided to go over and talk to you," I said.

"My friends kept asking me about you. They wouldn't shut up! I just told them 'Hey, I don't know, I just like the guy so far, and his name is Max, he's cute, let's see what happens.'"

"OK that's great. Misty's Coffee House. It's where I'd like to take you today. I've been there twice. It's very cool. I hope you'll like it. Five p.m. OK?" I asked.

"Yeah, sure."

"It's out there in the sticks. The quiet corner. A bit of a hike, but such a beautiful drive. I'll come pick you up?" I said, replaying the words in my mind. What did I just say. Did I actually say that? I could have worded that better. *What's wrong with me?*

"Yes, I'm OK with that. I'll text you my address. You should already know my town as we talked about that yesterday. Take care Max and see you later today. I'll be looking forward to it," she said.

Chapter 7

First Date with Kate. Coffee House

I suppose you could say I had a case of the butterflies before my date, but I knew I'd have to just get myself ready and look my best. What more could I do? Pick out a nice set of clothes, take another shower and why not work out beforehand. It always made me feel better. Something about shampooing your hair after a workout just felt better. I made an earl grey tea since I knew I'd have a coffee with Kate. I'd rather savor it then as opposed to the usual overkill of coffee I'd consume daily. This month has got to be about me. It's a time for change and what's all this about meeting Kate that night anyways I wondered. A sign, right? I mean, this has not happened to me in so long, and before that I met people online typically. But I was nervous now. Too nervous. But that's life, that's normal. But am I normal? Does she think I'm normal? She likes me so far, I can tell but how long will that last?

I splashed on some "Cool Water" cologne, something of the past that I found to be an intriguing scent which came in a blue rectangular glass bottle and a black top. I got dressed into a charcoal gray crewneck sweater, a pair of dark blue jeans, dark brown boots, glasses rather than contacts. I blow dried my hair then applied some of this product which had a beachy, rough texture that you mold your hair with. I was looking good but feeling nervous. Yet that's how I feel all too often, anyways. I better get going if I want to arrive at her place on time.

I picked Kate up and we headed east. Crossing the Connecticut River, we got into traffic. This slow-moving traffic made for good conversation time. I'd say some funny one-liners, just off the cuff, and she'd laugh, pretty hard. Was I wittier than I thought? Perhaps charming even. I'd been called that before. I just want to be me. Often at work I try to be myself but working at a hotel it's not always possible. When you've been working at the same place for at least five years, like me, you notice patterns in the work place. One lady quits and soon enough another is working with you who shares the same general personality as that previous co-worker. The same can be true for guys of course. Another pattern: when you've had two different managers tell you: "A little white lie won't hurt you at work to make your life easier." Or when at least two co-workers explain to you that they like to think of themselves on the job as "an actor on a stage." They have a point in some ways. I think you must act to show fake empathy for the guest who didn't get their foam pillows or good parking space. Otherwise you'd put yourself through emotional turmoil at the drop of a hat, always relating to the guests and "feeling their pain." Regardless, whatever you do, you're spent at the end of the day. You're spent at the *start* of the day. I'm searching for myself again during this month, the real me. Maybe she'd be a part of that process.

We arrived at the coffee house. Misty's was rare. A lot of local coffee shops could not compete with the big competition. And the ones which were around still? I could list the mistakes they were making. I'm not saying it would prevent me from going to them, but I notice these things. Little things I picked up on, like a Christmas soap dispenser in the bathroom during the month of May. Or just too much dust. Gift items for sale? I'd love to buy them but nothing on the shelf is grabbing my attention. They could improve if they would just put a little more thought and effort into it. I've seen these mistakes all too often, but Misty's was in another category altogether. They knew what they were doing. Even a room you'd walk into had actual mist in the air periodically. Now that's ambience. The colors were subtle but varied from purple to blue and red and all the rest. Live acoustic music was in progress as we arrived. A guy and gal singing on stage with guitar and keyboard. Her hair was almost long enough to reach her hips, yet the guy was bald. I guess she had to make up for his lack of hair. He wore a pair of thick framed black eyeglasses. They were playing an original number and introduced it by explaining how they came up with the lyrics. They were hiking at Sleeping Giant State Park and by the time they got back down to their car, it was completed.

We sat down at a table. I studied Kate's face without making it too obvious. Her features were just beautiful in my eyes… her nose, lips, but my cousins didn't think so. That was OK. She looked different and that's probably why I liked her. *I was different*, after all. I'd enjoyed her company tonight. We seemed to hit it off and we had great chemistry. Knock on wood. She had a dirty chai latte and I had a regular coffee, house blend, with milk, no sugar. We got up to get a refill. We were given mugs rather than paper cups. I enjoyed her perfume but didn't know how to describe it, other than to say it helped attract me to her even more so.

"So, I noticed you have a lot of patience when it comes to driving in traffic," she said.

"Thank you, well, sitting in a car with you, compared to being up all night at a hotel. I think I can deal with some traffic."

"So how do you stay awake all night?"

"Oh, that's something I got used to after the second or third night on, way back when I first started training."

"But you never sleep on the job, *right*?"

"Seriously Never. Some people out there *do,* but I couldn't. Just not my personality to try something like that. Did I tell you this past February, just a couple months ago, our fire alarm went off at two a.m.?"

"Was everything OK?" she asked.

"False alarm. Something about the water pressure or the sensor getting tripped up. I don't know but what I do know is that the alarm is loud enough to wake the dead. And when the phone kept ringing non-stop, I couldn't keep up with answering it, *obviously.* But when I *did* answer the phone my most common response was to say that yes, they would have to evacuate the building because until the fire department showed up, we'd have to treat the alarm as if it was real potential danger, for obvious reasons. But I'd remembered this same thing happening to me at least three times the previous year," I explained to Kate.

The duo continued to play music which served as a pleasant background soundtrack to our time at the coffee house. Then they played something I recognized and was thoroughly impressed with which was a cover of Toad the Wet Sprocket's "Walk on the Ocean." You've got to love that song.

"Well I have stories for you mister, but they are about my students and just your basic, run of the mill Christian school gossip. The rest of the staff have been pushing me to date again, so they'll get out of my hair once I tell them about you," she said.

"I have something for you," I told her.

"Oh really?"

I gave her the candle with the note. *Smart thinking Max*, I thought to myself while smiling. Her face lit up and she put her hand on my hand just for a second. She opened the gift and read the little note card smiling. Then she opened the cover from the large candle with her right hand holding the bottom of the candle with her left pretending it weighed a lot more than it did. Inhaling deeply as she put the wax near her nose. "Ahhh, I love it. Thank you!" I felt it was a good time to get up and look around, so I asked her to browse the place with me. It was her first time at this coffee house after all. We saw a couple of gift baskets for sale, tumblers, bags of coffee, spicy jam. Overall it was just a splendid night. I wanted everything to end on a positive note, so I thought, why not head home while things were going well.

We had a smooth drive back and the conversation turned to God. She wanted me to know she really liked me even though we are so new to each other. Being a Christian is the center of her life and in terms of dating, she'd expect the same from her man.

I got to talking to her about my background as a philosophy major and about college. How I'd said prayers in the recent past and how meeting her could be God's answer to those prayers. Sure, it was mushy, but I was being completely honest.

Our conversations continued along nicely. We approached her place and I pulled into her driveway. I kept the car running and as our conversations ended; it became awfully silent. The sense I got was that she wanted to tell me something, but she just got out and walked away after saying goodnight. She turned back around after she got halfway to her front door and approached my side of the car. I rolled down the window. "Would you like to come to Church with me for our next service?" she asked. Of course, I was delighted to and let her know it.

Chapter 8

Sunday Service with Kate

Everything was dandy with Kate. I loved her, although I only had seen her twice, and the first time was just that chance encounter by the lake, over beers. Of course, it was too soon to tell her exactly how strong I felt about her.

She came by to pick me up this time. I gave her a quick tour of my apartment, but of course I made sure to clean the place first, meticulously.

"Well, I don't want to be late," she remarked as we stepped outside and into her car. We made our way over to the Holy Covenant Church and I felt so happy and proud to be with her today. As she parked the car, I glanced over at her, not expecting her to notice me gazing at her eyes, but she did. I think she felt something special the way I did. It was evident in her expression.

I found myself almost in a Deja vu like experience, only because everything throughout the service was like another couple of churches I had already explored. I'd been handed a welcome bag which contained a pen inscribed with the message: The Lord is my Strength. Psalm 28:7. I thought, I'd use the pen at work to lift my spirits when I was tired and stressed. Then I remembered I didn't have to go to work for a long while. Thank God, Praise be to the Lord! They had a cafe in the front. Coffee, refreshments, a greeter, a newsletter handed to me with a warm greeting. "Welcome!!" It all seemed a little bit too fake for me. I don't know that she felt the same way or not, but I knew one thing: I'd listen, and I'd pray with an open mind and heart. And most of all it was her that I was just happy to be with. I suppose I only wished the Christian church services would take on a different style to some degree. Why not take the freedom to change the worship service from week to week and be more spontaneous and creative? Immediately upon entering the sanctuary we found a spot and just remained standing since the worship team had just struck the first chords of their opening song. Each person, for the most part, remained standing. Additionally, three more songs played and occasionally I glanced over at Kate appreciatively. She was dressed conservatively with a colorful sweater on and tan colored pants. Her socks were navy blue. I found the style she was wearing quite attractive. I guess the "leave more to the imagination" approach works for me. I also looked around the room to get an idea of who was there. It was a small church. I even counted the number of people in attendance, but lost count along the way.

We sat through the service, and I noticed some glances over in our direction. One older blonde lady with her husband, looking over at us, more often than a few times, made me feel like we were drawing attention, but in a good way. Kate was clearly a regular, but I on the other hand am brand new, so no wonder all eyes were on us.

The day continued on a high note as we stopped at an ice cream shop and restaurant which was near the church. It was one of those "been in business for fifty years" type of places. We ate lunch and discussed life and all. Kate, unlike myself, actually felt quite fulfilled in her career. She'd had the experience of attending private Christian schools all her life, so now that she taught at a private Christian school, on the elementary level, it was like a walk in the park for her.

"I never really knew what it was like to attend a public school," she said.

I felt she was lucky for that reason, but each has their own opinion. I felt invisible in my public school, mainly because it was so large; I was just a small fish in a big sea. I never got that close connection with everyone in the classroom, which I probably would have gotten in a smaller school. But as the saying goes, "The grass isn't always greener on the other side."

We agreed to see each other again, and once more parted ways on a high note. So far things were harmonious.

Chapter 9

Encountering Chen

Rolling out of bed I walked to the kitchen. Maybe someday I'd have the modern contemporary house that I've always wished for, or is it postmodern, maybe just contemporary. I don't know, but I'm happy to just be able to get out of bed in the *morning* rather than in the dark at night. As I sipped today's first cup of coffee, I let my thoughts tumble around my head. Then I made a focused effort at trying to recall last night's dreams. Nothing was coming to mind.

Kate and I were going well; I couldn't get her off my mind if I tried. I continued to think I was in love, so soon. I'd realized something. It was rare for me to meet someone, whether friend or girlfriend, that really connected to me. Someone who thought the way I thought. So, this made me think about an old friend Alan who was on my wave length. Kate sort of seemed to think the way I think. I made a strong connection to her at least. Now, this old friend I'm comparing her to, he was not particularly a good guy because of the way he'd stab you in the back. Yet he still thought the way I thought, take away most of the bad stuff. He'd tend to tell one friend something along these lines: "Max said such and such about you and oh by the way he thinks your car is a piece of junk too." Now, in reality, these are things I've never said. Yes, they were lies and that was the ugly side to this guy Alan. Somehow in his own twisted way, this old friend would talk behind each friend's back to create unnecessary enemies, and he also worked at creating enemies of people who were not even acquainted yet. That's the negative side but we still had that mastermind personality type in common. The ability to think deeply about every move in life as if it were a piece on the chessboard. The mastermind personality type is not a bad one, just often misunderstood. It can be used for good or for bad. My old friend did a little of both. I on the other hand steered clear of trouble. But Alan and I had a bond of sorts and Kate and I now had that bond, a connection where we felt comfortable together. In a sense, Kate has filled a void. I hadn't seen Alan in ten years and he's not online, so we just drifted apart. And now she gave me a jolt of electricity to light up my life. Combine that with coffee and you're on could nine.

I was in a searching mood. Yes, I'm a philosopher, but I was particularly in an exploring mood this morning. I headed out in the direction of some shopping centers and stopped in at Barnes and Noble across the way. Picking up a coffee from their café, I had a brief chat with the young woman who said her name was Michelle. I knew this "vacation" of mine was an opportunity for me to take initiative with being more outgoing so I talked more with Michelle. I learned she's originally from Thailand. Our conversation was pleasant. I had nothing in particular to buy so I headed over to the True Crime section. You can learn a lot from True Crime, like what mistakes not to make in life. Of course, experience is the greatest teacher and just reading about a manipulative man or woman might not be enough to keep you away from one but still the True Crime genre offers much. Take for instance something I've noticed. Just about 99% of all True Crime books deal with the same cause leading to murder: sexual immorality. It's not the only cause but it's the real cause. You can take that whatever way you like, but if you stop and think about it-people get jealous when someone cheats. Sooner or later that jealousy turns into rage and crime, for some people. Later I walked toward the Religion section. There I saw a softcover with glossy pages. A guide to world religions, cults, philosophies and groups. Leafing through the pages, I stopped when I came to the mother church of Boston belonging to Christian Science. I'd dabbled in their religion, once coming very close to signing up for membership. The posting in the main entrance to one of their churches in Connecticut listed a bunch of rules that each member would live by. I wrestled with those restrictions and rules for a few days until ultimately deciding it wasn't for me. The Seventh Day Adventists were another group I studied, but not too deeply.

I did find it surprising most of them practiced a vegetarian diet and went to church on *Saturday*. I'd always liked Saturday better than Sunday because as a kid I thought on Sunday you had to think about going back to that dreaded place otherwise known as school on Monday. As an adult you replaced the dreaded place called school with another dreaded place called work very often. But this next photo in the book got my attention. The building was modern and eclectic, displayed in full color. The caption read: Lawrence Espenschied Center, Warren, Connecticut. Built in 1986. A contemporary, award winning structure. Membership involves many aspects, for example: a full-sized gym, swimming pool and sauna….

An employee came by and asked me if I needed any help, startling me as I was lost in my reading. "I'm good, thank you, all set," I responded.

I looked up to the top of the page. Lawrence Espenschied Center. Lawrence "Larry" Espenschied grew in popularity at around the same time as his contemporaries, Tony Robbins, Brian Tracy. His organization grew from a grassroots demand of his fans. His book reached the best seller's lists and he worked with people one-on-one with dramatic results. His mission statement: People have emotional pain. Sometimes it's buried and sometimes it comes to the surface. I believe through total honesty we can share what's inside, to create a chain reaction of positivity on the outside. People will open more to you and you will open up more to them in return.... I kept reading further. The center's headquarters is in western Connecticut while other centers have cropped up over the years but died down most recently.... I personally didn't want to dig too deep in reading, for once in my life. Rather, I wanted to just jump right in. What could it hurt to take a drive there? After all, I was fortunate enough it was actually here in Connecticut. I stopped to think to myself. *You learn something new every day.*

I set my GPS to the location of the Center. Forty-seven minutes was reasonable, and I had all day. Still hadn't heard from Kate or anyone today yet. I was excited about the whole thing. Of course, not knowing if anyone would be there didn't matter. At least seeing this building up close was the equivalent of visiting an art museum, so I felt it worthwhile. Now I figured I'd known most of the state but certainly I could see how they hid a place like this among the rural parts of this section in Litchfield county. Not too hard to imagine.

As I drove closer, the GPS told me I had one minute to arrival. I didn't care for the gravel road, but soon I reached a smooth as silk driveway which appeared to be the entrance. A parking lot looked to be occupied by at least four cars. I pulled into a further off spot and walked up towards the building, but where was the front door entrance? I'd rarely seen anything so cool here in Connecticut. I'm sure they had buildings like this more commonly in Los Angeles no doubt, but this was rare. A spectacular conglomeration of geometric shapes, all very beautifully placed, here in the sticks of Connecticut? I walked towards the first triangular window I saw which was lower to the ground. I glanced inward and saw a reflection of someone sitting on a bench off behind me, slightly to my right. I turned and glanced over to him while still walking up towards the door, which I finally spotted upon further examination. Yes, the door was actually hard to find. Was this some kind of puzzle? I realized this must be the main entrance as I noticed a calendar of events. I reached for the handle and pulled the door towards me. Remarkably it was open. Glancing inward I felt a blend of nervous excitement and inner calm all at the same time. Maybe it was the order and design of what I saw which put me at ease; certainly, it was the "not knowing what was going to happen next" aspect which gave me the nervousness. I liked the soft blue colors, the palm plants inside the building, whether real or fake, made me feel more human and natural. I was beginning to think this break from work was the best thing that had ever happened to me. A circular fountain in the center of the lobby had a large formation of water gently bubbling. The sound was soothing. A scent was in the air. I recognized it as something like breezy ocean, or ocean breeze. The kind I use as incense or in a bubble bath. That was my interpretation anyways.

"Hi, welcome."

"Thank you, I responded... My first reaction to hearing her voice was that at least she didn't say: "What are you doing here? I'm calling the police!" It was a friendly greeting. I could sense it, most definitely. I glanced around, taking a few small steps, wondering what would happen next. Suddenly the phone rang, and I glanced off to my left turning around slowly, I saw a portrait photo on the wall. Was this Larry Espenschied, I wondered? Or perhaps another member of the church? Was it a church? For my sake I'd not think of it as a church until I knew otherwise. It's a self-help group? A personal improvement cult? Oh man that doesn't sound good. Hmm the man in the photo looked more like an accountant rather than some guru. In fact, it was Lawrence Espenschied, realizing his name underneath. A fit man, with curly hair, a dirty blond color, a bit of a receding hair line. A dynamite smile, a dark blue suit. This guy was charismatic. I could tell but I still hadn't even heard him speak. Just the building itself took on a life all its own.

"Sir, she politely spoke to me as I turned around flashing a slight smile, did you meet Chen? He's the man outside, there on the bench. Holding the phone to her shoulder, I can see she had to take the call, and wanted me to meet with this guy as she signaled him over, waving her free hand to him, so he can walk inside.

As the door swung open, he reached out a hand. "Hello, I'm Michael Chen, pleased to meet you. And you are?"

"Max, yes, nice to meet you also. Well, I'm here," I continued to speak, "to um well I was in the bookstore this morning first of all, and just happen to come across information about this group and then now here I am. But I never yet heard of this place and I'm rather impressed. I just thought I'd come here on my time off from work and take a look around," I fumbled for my words.

"Yes, sure that's something I can help you with. I'm in charge of giving tours and you picked a good time. Speaking of days off, I also have a day off today, and I'd like to show you around, although typically we do make appointments. Like I said, you just caught us at a good time. Follow me."

We walked down a hallway, above head, an arched narrow ceiling, all painted in various subtle colors. Around a corner, we turned, and there were streams of water on our sides. I could hear them, babbling brooks, if you will. Sort of like man-made waterways with plants surrounding. A mural painting of a natural landscape along the wall to my left depicted a great blue heron.

Michael had showed me the workout facility, sauna, auditorium, and various other parts of the building. The more I saw, the more I had a sense of wonder. It was like nothing else I'd ever experienced outside of Disney World or the Creation Museum for that matter. One spiral staircase led to a room I had no idea about; another led to yet another, without any explanation. Did the leader of this group live here? "Where do all these spiral staircases lead to Michael?"

"Where *don't* they lead to! Call me Chen by the way, if you'd like anyways," he said.

"Ok well, thank you Chen."

"So, this is our center," Chen responded with a half-smile.

"It's beautiful. I work in a hotel. Often, people walk in, glance around, and say our place is beautiful. But as for me, night after night, seeing the hotel, I'm bored pissless, pardon my French. I suppose the hotel just doesn't come near the style of design I'm seeing here. Beauty is in the eye of the beholder, no doubt, but I just know that whoever designed *this* place, has got my kind of taste, must be a kindred spirit," I remarked.

"Well, Lawrence himself, Mr. Espenschied helped in the design and layout for sure. That was a long time ago. Speaking of jobs, I work in insurance. It's something I'm trying to escape, but the pay is reasonable. In addition, I work here for Larry, and working towards making a transition to full time employment within the Center. Tell you the truth, that's my dream."

"Funny you mention it. I'm looking to escape my line of work also. Easier said than done. At least now I'm on a one month 'hiatus', and part of the reason I'm here, at this center today, in the first place is that I'm trying to take more chances. Open myself up to more things.

"Let's take a seat," Chen said.

We sat down, and I found myself just opening to what Chen was saying, and before I knew it I had spent a lot of time listening internally nodding my head to all I was hearing. I found out much over the course of the next fifteen minutes as we talked.

Chen continued to speak. We work our way upward in levels and we have little celebrations here in our auditorium for each one who rises to each level but soon the levels stop, and we are all on the same level, but the rest of the journey, I'm told, is just as much fun as it was when we first begin.

"How do you mean? I asked.

"Well, like… Larry feels that it takes a certain point of understanding, where each person can climb up and reach new levels of healing or improvement. But at a certain point, he feels you've reached a sufficient standing in life. In the beginning you're a level one but you can go up to five. At that point, do you still have some room to grow? Sure, but you don't need to reach a level six.

"What do you mean, exactly?

"There is no level six, which is good because, then there's no more hierarchy with exception to Larry. He's the CEO and he's the founder…sure he's also the sort of "pope" when it comes to the doctrine of what we're doing but he strongly feels that once you get to a level five you're at a point where he knows that you know what this group is generally all about. The rest is up to you. You learn, you grow, you communicate and have friendships with all of us, but you don't reach a higher level on paper. The other thing that Espenschied feels strongly about is physicality. He knows that if you're not happy, you're most likely struggling with being overweight in so many cases," Chen said.

"It's true, I can see that," I said.

"I'll let you in on a secret. When I refer to these levels as number one, two, etc., it's a simplification because there are also fancy esoteric names for stuff within Larry's teachings. And the other part of the secret I'll let you in on is that lately he's been considering re-structuring the whole system. Getting rid of the levels and fancy names. I think it's because he doesn't want people to think of him as some kind of guru or Christ like figure. There's really a deeper reason also. I think personal struggles have led him to re-evaluate his life. I don't know why I'm telling you all this but I'm just an honest guy. You didn't hear it from me!" Chen explained.

"So, we have a gym here, but you don't have to work out here. But we've got one and we work on that. It's part of the level system. If you've reached a level five here, then you've come to grips with where you are at with your body. You've been able to do what you want as far as getting to your ideal weight if that is something you're after. If it isn't, then that's OK, but that stuff is talked through in our group sessions." Chen continued and again I listened rather intently.

It turns out I enjoyed talking to him very much. I found myself on the same wavelength as him, quite comfortable. I felt a mutual respect that was quite palpable. I didn't get that with people staying at my hotel or even co-workers necessarily. I'd been fortunate to get along with all my co-workers but too often they'd turn around and whisper something to another co-worker trying to scheme about something silly. My luck was strong this week. Romantically with Kate, and friendship wise with Chen. I can tell that he was someone who would stay in mind and as far as I was concerned I'd become a part of this whole thing. I couldn't resist. On the one hand I'd become over saturated with self-help and world religions especially now that I've become a Christian, exclusively. But on the other hand, this place didn't really fill the description of a religion or anything demonic or suspect for that matter. It was mainly the intriguing beauty and mystique of the place that grabbed a hold of me.

"You see max, I grew up heavy and it's not only that. My parents are immigrants, from Asia, and that's great and fine but some of the kids in school took advantage of making fun of my weight and different culture. Rather than celebrating what I brought to the table, a bit of diversity, they pounced on me. I didn't like growing up where I did, here in Connecticut, and I always wished things would be different. I didn't grow up somewhere like here out in a quiet town in the sticks but, just a typical average Connecticut town," he said.

Observing Chen, I saw he was fit enough for sure. The man had clearly overcome whatever weight issues he'd faced as a youth. We both were shy, particularly in our younger years, and I found we were about the same age now in our 30's. He was fast becoming a great friend in such a short period of time. Who else has shared so many details so quickly. And personal details, very personal.

Chapter 10

Spiritual Experiences

Laying down in bed, I felt a heavy sleepiness come over me. It was only three or four in the afternoon, but after all, I must have still felt the pull of the night shift routine. So why fight it? I'll just take a catnap, I figured. I drifted off, not yet asleep, I lay there halfway between wakefulness and dreaming. I heard a buzzing sound which I also felt subtlety pulsing through me, then I was lifted in the air. Not literally, but in my imagination, as I floated there for a minute I then shot back to reality and got out of bed knowing for sure I was never fully asleep, nor was I fully awake. All the while I saw a green-blue light in the distance, such as a beam which later focused into a single point. The beam then disappeared.

What had just happened? Chen was speaking to me about spiritual experiences at the Center. He'd spoken about lights and sounds and sensations. He was honest enough to say he'd not experienced all those things but that some people have claimed to have experienced them and attributed thanks to Larry's organization. They'd even written a couple books on their experiences. I've done plenty of exploring before this and I've meditated. I've done yoga, church, prayers, energy work. For sure, many things. This was cool. This was good, so I think anyways.

I decided I'd give him a call. Maybe we'd get a chance to take a drive and hang out at the casino or something. A far drive would give us a chance to talk.

Chapter 11

Casino with Chen

Stepping inside the casino I noticed a scent which brought back memories as far ago as my teenage years. I'd been here with family and friends, way back then, but not to gamble, rather to hang out in the under 21 section, where they had attractions, virtual reality type rides and such. The scent I noticed was sweetgrass mixed with perhaps balsam fir and lavender, yet it also had tobacco as many people smoked throughout the casino. Now, to me the scent of cigarette smoke wasn't bothersome because it reminded me also of the arcade in my town as a kid. Walking through the hallway, I passed a gift shop to my left. I peeked in from the outside glass spotting coffee mugs, ash trays, caps all bearing the casino's logo. I didn't really have time to waste as I was going to meet up with Chen for seven p.m. by the entrance to one of their theatres. I was disappointed I couldn't just car pool with him since the drive here always feels so painfully long, but he had something important to attend to, leaving me scratching my head about it all. But hey, it's OK. Glancing at my watch, I saw that I was five minutes early.

Walking towards the doors to the theatre, I saw him already standing there glancing at his cell phone. "Hey buddy, what's up?!" I yelled out.

"Not too much, it seems we're both rather punctual people," he responded with a small laugh.

"You know, this is cool. I haven't done much of anything like this lately, I responded. I work nights, I go home, I veg out in front of the computer, all too often, and when the weekend comes around, I find myself repeating the same routine to the point where I begin to wonder what else to do. Don't get me wrong; I've gone to places like this over the years, but then I begin to question if it's worth going all by myself so often. For a few years, it *was* worth it, but then the drive got awfully long, and I found the sense of nostalgia wearing off. Maybe you can relate to what I'm saying?" I said.

"I've only been here about twice Max. Once, for a show, right here, where we are standing, in front of this theatre. I saw Collective Soul. I got into their music just randomly when I heard a song online, didn't realize then how great their catalog of music is."

"Love that guys voice," I said.

"Ed, Ed Rolland, very cool. He's inspired by an 80's sound like The Cars, especially. Older stuff too, like the Beatles, Elton John, but what they do is underappreciated, really," Chen said while rubbing his chin.

"I agree."

We continued walking at a brisk pace, enjoying the lively crowd all around us. I personally wouldn't come here alone on a Friday or Saturday night. Tonight, is a Friday night so having at least someone along made things a whole lot different, and it really struck me again how out of touch I've gotten in the social realm. But now with Chen, albeit, a brand-new friend, Kate, also new, but so exciting, things have come together in an amazing and virtually indescribable way.

Lost in thought, as we walked, Chen jolted me out of my day dream by tapping me on my shoulder with the back of his hand while saying, "Your cousins?"

"Huh?" I responded.

"Your cousins, Sally, Robert? They're supposed to be here tonight you mentioned? Chen said while we both stopped walking and leaned up against the wall.

Yes, now this was another thing that sort of irked me about them, I thought to myself. They said they'd be here after seven or later; they'd text us. We planned to stop for a drink at the club with them, do a little gambling. But still, no word from them.

"I'll let you know Chen. When they text me; we'll meet up with them. They're *notorious* for being late, plus I haven't really been in contact with them much lately," I said.

We walked towards an exhibit and stopped to look. It was of Native Americans and in a natural setting. Something which reminded me of a childhood trip I took to the Boston Museum of Science. The detail and artistry were quite remarkable. Sounds of nature were in the background. A rainstorm, thunder, wind and the sound of birds. Chen folded his arms and looked carefully.

"Very cool Max! I've never seen this before. I must have entered by the other entrance when I'd come here before," he said.

We walked away from the exhibit casually. I said while pointing my finger in the distance, "Hey, let's go this way." As we walked, we passed underneath a rock formation, while a waterfall flowed overhead it to our left.

"I'd love a coffee." I said

"Yeah, that sounds good."

Walking into the cafe I smelled the tempting pastries and glanced behind the counter. Massive blueberry muffins, ginormous black and white cookies, biscotti, cheese and spinach bread rolls. Steam was coming off the espresso machine as a young, blonde haired woman, worked on crafting a beverage. Her shiny hair flowed out of her baseball cap. There was a warmth in the air. And a mist. Chen got in line, but I got distracted glancing behind me. I'm a sucker for gift items. I picked up a small rainstick and turned it upside down. I liked the worldbeat style of music playing in the café, but I couldn't place what it was. I took a deep breath through my nose and noticed a fragrance in the air. Somehow it called upon my memory banks and I felt like a teenager again. Must have been something about that scent to conjure feelings of romance. Juniper I believe, it was a cool and relaxing scent.

"You want me to get you something while you look around?" Chen turned around and yelled out to me.

"Yesssirrrr," I said it all in one word enthusiastically, "coffee, medium, extra milk, no sugar. Thank you." The medium could have been medium roast or medium size. It didn't matter to me at that moment.

I slowly walked along the side of the café. An assortment of green plants was along the base of the frosted glass. I glanced over at the line; Chen was waiting behind two people. I checked my phone, still no text messages from the cousins. Wait a minute, I thought, didn't they get rid of those rocks and waterfall years ago? Am I confusing the two casinos? No, can't be. That bookstore I saw, wasn't it out of business last time I was here? I'd never even been in this café. But I liked it. I *really* liked it. This is what the casino *should* look like. For reasons beyond me the executives gradually made changes to the already wonderful appearance. I suppose to make the place look more modern and compete with the other casinos. Still with each new change they made, I became less and less interested in visiting. Still my memories lived on. Memories like when I was only sixteen years old, visiting with a neighbor and his parents. Playing video games and all sorts of attractions which are also no longer here. Chatting it up with girls we'd found, albeit we had no luck that day. We didn't need to gamble. Still I don't need to gamble to enjoy this place. Sure, twenty dollars on the slots are worthwhile. After all, if you lose: no big deal. If you win big, then great.

Chen had two cups in his hand, plus two honey sticks in his mouth. He handed me my coffee and he took a big gulp of his extra-large cappuccino.

"Is that honey stick for me?" I asked realizing it had been in his mouth already.

"Peppermint and lemon flavored. Just open it from the other end. You suck the honey out of it like a straw. My hands were full!" he said.

"I know how it works Chen, I used to get honey sticks like these as a kid from Rogers Orchards," I told him.

Without having to discuss where we'd sit, we both just walked out of the café and decided upon a bench to sit at down the hall. Nobody was around this area much. Everyone was much too busy rushing around on the more familiar beaten path.

I sipped my coffee slowly. "Chen, you know, at the Center…there are these rooms up higher where you see windows but you're inside all the while. They're not hotel rooms, are they?"

"Oh no, not hotel rooms," he responded, "but what about your cousins? I'd like to meet Sally."

"At this point, they're pretty late. I think maybe they're playing games with me. You know, I overhead them talking about Kate. Saying she had an ugly nose. I think her nose looks attractive Chen. That was behind my back. But in person they criticized her to me also. Very superficial. It's like family thinks they know what's best for you or *who* is best for you. But if they knew what was best for you they'd actually just let you live your life."

"Oh, I see," he said taking another sip of his cappuccino.

I changed the subject by asking, "How about that lady at the center in the tight black pants, you remember? She was doing those stretches in the gym when you gave me the tour. You know who…."

"That's Yu-Jin, she's half Korean. I fooled around with her," Chen said.

"What? You *fooled* around with her? She was *really* cute Chen," I said.

"Yeah. I know," he responded.

"But I don't agree with that. I just think fooling around like that is not the way to go…" I began.

"And Kate?" Chen asked.

"Kate and I are not fooling around Chen. We're both devoutly Christian. It's just part of our way of life. Everyone is free to do what *they* want, but I know the difference between right and what I feel is wrong," I explained to him.

"Hmmm." He looked down at the floor then re-tied his shoe laces.

"Back to those windows in the Center…I thought if they were hotel rooms then there'd be an opportunity for me to work there with my experience in the industry, but it seems…" I began to say.

"You know what I *do* know Max?…I saw something…"

"What'd you see?" I asked.

"Don't tell anybody! OK? Let me set the mood for you. You know when it's beginning to get dark outside and someone flips on the light. The soft yellow glow in a room. I was sitting there on that white, smooth bench where you'd see all those windows. Maybe this is the same place you were just asking me about at the Center. I don't know. The Center is a bit of a maze. But regardless, I was sitting there, inside the building mind you, and those windows happen to be in the distance. A few of them were lit up with that warm glow of light and so I gazed up at them. I saw Larry's wife. Undressing. I wasn't there for that reason. I don't even know what those rooms are for. Who'd have thought his wife would be there anyways.

"What?"

"Yes, she had on tight blue jeans. Long legs, she's beautiful. She'd taken them off. But I didn't see enough if you know what I mean. She has dark curly hair, like Andie MacDowell," he said.

"I would look also Chen. How could you *not* look?" I said. "I certainly don't have that kind of willpower… to turn my eyes away."

"The curtain was open. On purpose? I don't think so. People are careless like that, I suppose," he said.

"Wow. Well your story is wild Chen," I said, shaking my head.

"What scares you about work Max?" he asked.

"Scares me? Well where do I begin? I can tell you this; last month I got strange phone calls. The guy was calling from an outside line. We don't have caller ID at the hotel, but I knew it was not from inside one of our hotel rooms. He asked about his check out date. Said he was going over his paper work. So, he was at home or in his car for instance. I'd asked him what his room number was. Because a room number is a personal piece of information. Think about it Chen; do you know, at this precise moment, the hotel room number of someone, anyone? Probably not. Unless it's your family member, wife or girlfriend who'd be out on business or something. So, this guy didn't know his room number, because he didn't have one, and the name he gave me did not match any name checked into our system, nor did it match a name due to check in or a cancellation even. It would have been just a little odd but then it got scary because he continued to call the next night also. He's probably trying to get to someone. Maybe he's a jealous ex-boyfriend. A real sinister sounding son of a bitch, but these are true stories Chen, not just the workings of my imagination here, scary stuff, aggravating stuff that really happens. You've got to deal with it," I said.

"What scares *you* about work Chen?" I returned the question to him.

"Hartford traffic. If Mark Twain could see it now. He'd be turning in his grave. The customers on the phone. Insurance is not a business I belong in Max," he responded with a look of disgust on his face.

Next, I sat up slowly. Gathering my thoughts. My mind unraveling what had just happened. I was *dreaming*. It was all a dream. The casino with Chen. If I had a note pad by my bed, I'd write everything down, but I didn't. My cousins. They'd not stood us up but rather it was all in my head. I still was pissed about my cousins. Who the hell were they to disapprove of Kate? And then they were snickering about her religious beliefs as well. And they did criticize the way her nose looked. Here I was dreaming about it even. It's as if some people have this preconceived definition of what beauty looks like. But it doesn't work like that for me. I'd had just about enough of those idiots. I'd glanced over at my cell phone on the night stand. Two AM illuminated in the dark room. Suddenly my cell phone text message went off, jolting me a bit. It was Kate. Hi, thinking about you. Don't want to bother you now but just had to say Hello!!:)<3. Wondering if we can see each other again??...

Chapter 12

Getting a Taste of Something New

Things were moving along quite beautifully, albeit *strangely*, on my one-month sabbatical, if you want to call it that. Strange, but a beautiful kind of strange. New friends, new relationships, powerful, vivid dreams. It's not that I didn't have other friends. Randall Christopher, an old friend going back fifteen years, has been on vacation in Denmark with his parents. He'd be gone for another three weeks.

While I'm proud to have him as a friend all these years, the frustration of our friendship had felt like being on a dead-end road stuck in the mud. Every time I'd try to convince him to attempt dating someone, he'd never take the plunge. I'd wondered if he had any attraction to women or to men for that matter. He seemed to be permanently stuck in life, but he also didn't seem to care that he was stuck either. Usually I'd ask God how to help me deal with my friendship with him rather than resorting to labelling him the wrong way. Perhaps with him on vacation I'd been able to open the door to different friends and possibilities. But I hoped that when he returned, I'd be able to introduce him to Chen, Kate, the Center even. Trying to invite him to a Christian service didn't do any good after all. He'd not cared enough to attend or was it an irrational fear.

Suddenly my phone vibrated in my pocket. It was Chen. Pleased to get his text, I was curious to see what he wanted. Come by the temple this afternoon. 5 PM, it's something I was able to get you in free for. A workshop we're doing.

I texted him the following: Sure, buddy I'm down for that AND I had a dream, you're going to want to hear this. It's about the casino. It's like a premonition? Well, we'll talk. see you at 5.

I found myself with a couple hours on my hand, so I decided to get some fresh air and take a jog right outside my apartment. I wondered why Chen called Larry's center a "temple" but then again after all my new age and religious explorations, the word temple was one hundred percent commonplace to me. I got dressed into something comfortable. A Montpelier Vermont sweatshirt and running pants. I built up a sweat after just ten minutes and admired some of the houses along the way. Something about walking or jogging that allows you to notice the little details you miss when driving. The more intricate doors and windows for instance. I stopped to admire my favorite plant, the dusty miller. I just loved that combination of colors, green and white, plus it was fuzzy and looked like snow. It felt good to pick up the pace and burn some more calories. Maybe it would also calm me down and take the edge off that I might feel at the workshop. Just being around mostly new people tends to make me anxious. I think Chen will help with that as we've gotten along well so far.

I'd arrived early at the Center, before five p.m. I noticed Chen in the parking lot. Ran up to him and gave him a pat on the back. He'd scanned his ID at the front entrance and helped me through, explaining I had a "free pass per Larry."

"Larry wasn't here today," he told me, but the session would be led by Dr. Rosenstein.

"Larry's not a doctor, right?" I asked.

"No, he's not. This guy Rosenstein's a psychologist in New Fairfield but what he does here he does here. And what he does in his private practice is based on what he does here. I'm simplifying things, of course but you get what I mean," Chen explained.

"I think so, Interesting," I responded.

We'd gathered in the auditorium, the doctor led us there and shook my hand before we made our way into the large space, introducing himself. Rosenstein climbed up the few stairs leading to the stage. "We could have used the classroom space down the hall. But I don't know, I just like this auditorium. Maybe it's because it's an open space and we need to air our feelings out into the open," he explained. On he went for another five minutes getting right to the point. We'd been then broken up into groups of three. Chen was with me because I was just a visitor. Karen was grouped with the two of us.

Chen whispered over to me, "I know her Max; she's nice."

I was beginning to think Chen knew everyone in the Center, which would be a bonus for me if I'd join. It potentially meant a good crowd to network with. I'd felt comfortable talking to Chen about anything, but a third person, a stranger, would make anyone apprehensive. Our assignment entailed very personal detail sharing. Details of our life. We'd all dispersed to different locations which were written on our index cards. We'd gotten "Board Room 3" so that's where we headed. Of course, Chen knew how to find it. The instructions were very simple, and we went through basic talking exercises which got deeper and deeper. I sat back in my comfortable office chair and swiveled left and right letting my back sink into the soft padding of the chair. After a while things got kind of heavy as Karen was crying and even shaking while going into detail about an abusive relationship she'd gone through. I'd understood how this form of therapy was productive because we'd got to make connections with people face to face and help each other out. The questions were written out on paper and we'd followed through with what we were instructed to do. Much of it was open ended and we'd be able to take things in different directions also.

Chen was speaking about a difficult time in his past. "This one time, I was at a real low point. Age fifteen, sophomore year in high school. You see, at home my family was dysfunctional, but I never thought of it that way necessarily, because it was all I knew. Plus, there were no drugs or much alcohol in the home, neither yelling for that matter. But a lot of things were just bottled up inside, and I later learned in life how that isn't healthy. My weight was high, and I didn't know how to get it down. At home there was no support in that regard plus at one point I'd started making some progress with exercise and my own mother told me that I'd never completely lose all the weight because 'it's in your genes,' she'd said. 'You'll always be that way,' she added. Of course, that's ignorant thinking but back then I just felt bad hearing it. So, one particular morning, in between classes at school, I was walking through the hallway and a popular kid whom never spoke to me before, because I'd never had a class with him, saw me walking in his direction. Nobody else was in the halls at that moment. He yelled out 'Fat Shit' and just continued on his way. I felt terrible. I'd wake up some mornings and just be depressed, thinking even this guy who doesn't know me is judging me in the hallways. What could I do about it? This was me; this was my identity. What else did I have? My school life was bad. My home life was bad. I had no support system. And this popular kid who'd insulted me: who's to say he wouldn't just punch me out the next time he saw me for no reason at all? Add being scared to the list of feeling depressed. And I was desperate for a girlfriend. But that wasn't going to happen anytime soon. You can see how people struggle with self-esteem. We're not all brought up the same way."

"I can relate to having been a bit of a loner Chen, but the other stuff, I don't know if I can relate to."

"That's it Max, that's just it. When I try to explain to people the difficulties I've had growing up they all say something which doesn't resonate with me. Like "that wasn't so bad, you should hear this," and then they'll relay to me something which they've gone through or some other terrible thing they heard about from someone else.

"Give me an example," I said.

"Take for instance the weight thing. In and of itself, there are challenges with the weight issue and people are aware of that; but weight is just weight. For example, there was a kid heavier than me growing up in class, but he was a popular kid. And you know why? He probably had a family that got involved in the community. Me, I was not just a loner, but my family were loners also. A foreign family in America with parents not involved in the community and not there to get involved in your life either. I can go on with this, but you get the idea. You must consider mental illness in the home also.

Karen nodded her head, agreeing with Chen. "I can relate to what you're saying Michael, there was mental illness in my family. But it wasn't something you talked about with everyone. It was just swept under the rug. But that's not fair to the kids."

"And you could list all these problems I've been talking about guys, but there are even more issues with the way I looked," Chen added.

"Like how? Karen asked keeping in mind the approach to questions we were supposed to take. The idea was to get our inner thoughts out into the open so that we'd be comfortable with them.

"I had cosmetic issues; birthmarks, I was very self-conscious. You know, around that same time I was speaking about before; age fifteen is when it was the worst. But nobody in my family said anything. It still makes me wonder to this day about why they didn't help me out with that. But I myself got fed up with things. I had this dream you know, one night when I rubbed my face and the birth marks just fell off and I had a normal face without the birthmarks and it was a cool dream Max. Then I woke up and it wasn't real but still at least the dream was something.

"Like a foreshadowing?"

"Exactly, that's right because when I finally did go to the dermatologist he took care of it for me very easily and then my life was different after that. It was also around this same time that I started losing weight. Maybe that's what I needed to get the ball rolling. Next thing you know, I'd lost twenty-five lbs. or so and was approaching my junior year in high school.

"What a difference a year makes," Karen said.

"Yes," Chen responded, "but it's that way when you're young. A short period of time seems longer and now time goes by quickly and we go on for so long without doing enough."

"It's like that with me and my hotel job; I want out but feel stuck," I added.

"And I the same with my insurance job in Hartford; I think soon it will be over and I'll come work here at the Center. The anticipation is killing me though, I need to know now but I'm just afraid to confront Larry or put pressure on him. He's mentioned it, but he wasn't completely direct about it.

I started thinking about what Chen was saying. I found myself torn between the Center and the Christian church I'd been to with Kate. I don't know if both will be compatible, yet I don't see why they couldn't be. Some people attribute most of the self-help gurus out there with an anti-Christian perspective. Also, yoga and the martial arts can be classed as anti-Christian according to several experts on the subject. One argument for this is that they are relying on a spiritual energy that is not of God. God of the Bible that is. This conversation among the three of us went on for another hour. We'd all meet back up again in the auditorium. Upon leaving I shook Karen's hand and told her 'thank you.' It was a pleasure to meet her and the three of us had shared so much and opened up to each other. Maybe the Center was a place for serious people who cared about each other.

Not everyone has the compassion out there. I know a lot of people talk about anti-bullying and sticking up for people in need. But it's been my observation that some of the people who put on a big show about it are really the same jerks who were obnoxious and trouble makers back when they were in high school. Don't believe everything you read online. People can talk a lot but then lose their patience and get angry with you. Bullying takes on a lot of different forms. Sometimes it's passive aggressive or condescending. I can't say I understand it all, but I think often it has to do with needing to be in control. There's also a wise saying I heard once: Hurt people hurt people.

As for me, I was going to tell them a story about a lady who I'd checked into my hotel last year. She'd come back fifteen minutes later and slammed her key cards on the front desk. She'd been mad because I gave her a room that was next to the elevator. A room like this is not necessarily a bad thing. She'd **not** requested one away from the elevator. Some people actually want rooms next to the elevator. But she was not having it. She was angry, furious, almost crying, and practically having a nervous breakdown. I suppose a little bit of noise from the elevator can do that to you. It was late, sure. She probably had a long day. Maybe something in her personal life was going bad. She'd been at my hotel visiting her kid in the nearby prep school. Very expensive prep school I'll add. But I was also a victim to the time of night. I'd have to be up all night and not be able to go to sleep like her. Yet she took out all her frustrations on me. It takes a toll. It's hard to always be the punching bag. I didn't tell this story to Chen and Karen today after I'd seen Karen shake and cry telling her story. Instead I just told them about how I felt I deserved more respect from my classmates as a kid. I'd felt tired of always being left out. I suppose if I never heard Chen or Karen speak so personally about their lives I would have not spoken about personal details from my life. One person admits that their life is not so perfect and all of a sudden, it's easier to do the same yourself. *What a concept.*

Chapter 13

Conversations with Kate

Kate and I had another date lined up and of course my schedule was free as can be. Luckily, she was off work because of a student field trip which she was not required to attend because she fulfilled the requirements the previous year, serving as a chaperone. I was happy to have this time with her. Thus far, standing near her gave me the so-called butterflies, in a good way. And I can sense Kate's interest in me was like a strong magnetic force. I hope it lasts.

This time I'd drive. She had never been to the outlets by the shore, so I convinced her quite easily to come along for a drive with me. I slowly drove up her street, as not to miss the house, and pulled into her driveway. She was standing outside wearing a pair of jeans, which tightly hugged her body, a gray fleece, zipped up to the top, along with a yellow pocketbook in her right hand.

"Right on time!" she yelled out right after I rolled down the passenger side window.

"I can see you're wasting no time," I responded as I made the quick, and probably smart decision, to jump out of the car and walk around to her side to open the door for her.

We pulled out of her driveway and I slowly descended the steep hill to glance at the houses and take in the moment. We passed a couple side roads until I saw the entrance to route 9 south on our right.

"You really know your way around here,

don't you?" she asked with a smile in her voice.

"Actually, I just kind of know Connecticut like the back of my hand. It's not that I know *this* area any more than say Berlin, Farmington, Waterbury, or Hamden. I just know most of the main arteries. Often, on my days off, a couple years back, I got into cruising around aimlessly, and I got to study a lot of routes. The Connecticut wine trail for instance. Very scenic, no matter if you're in the Quiet Corner or the Litchfield Hills etc. etc. It all has Its charm," I responded.

Route 9 is scenic, it's not as crazy as 84 or 15, out in Fairfield County. The cars give you a little bit more breathing room, if you're lucky. Route 2, heading towards the casino, is similar. Not a lot of buildings on the side of the road. Just a whole lot of pine trees, some streams and ponds. I once saw a woodchuck standing by the side of the highway, upright, eating an apple with both hands. But I was just happy to be with her in the car, because frankly I had gotten tired of going on my own, and old friends just kind of faded away years ago. Some of these old friends wanted to reconnect with me in recent years, sending me messages on Facebook but I'd felt some of them didn't have the moral character that I was looking for. I'm not saying I was morally superior, but I think you've got to treat people the way you want to be treated and show kindness. Sure, they would have been kind to me but then talk horrendously about the next guy behind their back. It's a kind of superficiality plus if I left the room, odds are they'd say something negative about me. Another thing I saw was lacking in our society was a thirst for knowledge from books. But now I had *her*, and I also had this new-found best friend Chen, who, like me, perhaps is a bit of a loner, so it seemed. I wondered if one day Kate, Chen and myself would all get together. Well, not *if*, but *when* because things were better than they had been in a long while for me, and I had a feeling all pieces of the puzzle would fall into place.

I noticed, out of the corner of my eye, Kate was flipping through my CD case.

"You don't mind if I look through here, dooo you?" she accentuated some of her words as usual.

"No, not at all."

"I'm going to pick something out, Ohhkaay?"

I glanced in my rearview mirror, noticing nobody directly behind me and another car zooming by in the left lane, while I kept a steady pace heading a few miles over the speed limit. No hurry today, I thought.

"Dog's Eye View? Hmmm," she said while inserting the disc into my stereo.

"It's their second album 'Daisy'; I think it failed to sell many copies, but it's almost as good as their debut album. I just think they represent a piece of the 90s especially," I said.

The music started playing and I adjusted the volume a couple notches lower, so it was at a comfortable level. "They sound like Matchbox Twenty which I'll admit is a good band, however, Dog's Eye View is still different yet because the singer, Peter Stewart, gets expressive, stretching his voice in all kinds of ways a little out of the ordinary. Meanwhile the band jams which sort of puts me in a trance. I suppose it's hard to put my finger on it. Sometimes I'll just start listening to their music and I won't want to listen to anything else the whole rest of the week," I explained.

"We're almost there," I said.

"Good, because I have to pee," she responded.

A sign for East Haddam and the opera house was up ahead. We drove on for another ten minutes or so and got off to take the rest of the way by back roads. I was telling Kate all about the differences between the two main outlets by the shore; one a little fancier but somehow, I liked the outlets which were further east, better. They also had a movie cinema. We passed lobster stands and seafood restaurants. The sense that we were in a beach town was made apparent by the scent in the air as I rolled down the windows a tad. We both inhaled at about the same time. Then we started laughing.

Arriving at the outlets, we walked through the parking lot and Kate glanced at me. Our eyes made contact. She walked up beside me, pressed her arm against mine which gave me a clear enough signal that I'd be OK holding hands with her. So, I reached over and did just that. I loved the feeling of her hand in mine. We walked by a bath and soaps outlet, then the bakery.

"There, I see a bathroom over there. I'll be right back. Can you wait for me here?" she said. I glanced around and rested my forearm along a wood beam. I watched the goings-on for a couple minutes and then she came out and said. "I like that smell in the air, fresh bread."

"It's nice. I wish they still had that little bookstore here," I mentioned.

" So, what are you thinking?" she asked looking right at me again.

"Oh nothing."

"You look deep in thought."

"I guess I'm always thinking and that's just something people might notice about me. I think that it's just the way I am, but I've also kind of learned to be aware of it. You know I used to work at the mall, ages ago. I had this coworker who'd tell me I looked perplexed. It's interesting Kate, because, of course, back then I got frustrated internally when I'd hear him say that, but I didn't know what to say in return, *so* I didn't say much. It's an open-ended statement almost like a question, so I don't really know if it seemed to him that I was perplexed about something on the register at work, in my personal life or whatever. Being able to communicate is the key, but socially I was lacking in some capacity. You've got to be able to conversate and resolve things. I just didn't have that at home growing up. Neither did Chen, probably that's why we get along. We can relate to each other. It's good that these things happen in life because then we know what kind of body language we are giving off. I'm just a thinker and I'm an introvert also," I said.

"I like the way you are Max; I like you *a lot,* so if you're going to change or improve yourself in anyway just check with me first!" she said.

We looked around some stores and later sat down in the corner on a wooden ledge. A small Japanese pine tree and fresh mulch beside us. She talked about her school, which she taught at. Kate had been successful at not joining in with the gossip but just about everyone else had gotten sucked into it. The principal was rumored to have had an affair, but within the past year, all talk about it had ceased. It was because word got out that the rumor was completely false. It gave renewed meaning to the phrase "You can't believe everything you hear."

Kate looked at me and began to say, "Since I've met you I feel more complete, because, yes, my work has been fulfilling and family life, church and all have been great but now, it's clear to me that God has answered my prayers when it comes to meeting someone, *romantically*. And it's not easy for me to tell you all this, being so personal that is, but I feel comfortable saying almost anything to you Max, because you are different. I want to know more about you and I want you to be happy."

"I think work just plain kills me Kate, it's like a slow death."

"Give me some examples of how," she began to say.

"Well… just take for instance, um, like where do I begin? Maybe the broken elevator last year or I don't know, the criminals who've smashed in the windows of the cars in the parking lot who had left their Christmas shopping in plain sight on their back seat. There are so many examples I can talk about, but let's just say, a typical night might go as follows: Imagine you come into work and it's 75% full, which is not even *that* busy, relatively speaking. Now stick with me here. A family was sitting in the lobby, at our restaurant, finishing up their drinks and playing cards. Our lobby and restaurant are all out in the same open space, by the way. They are here visiting a local college. You pretty much block them out of your awareness since you must focus on your arrivals, due to show that night. You have nine arrivals left still, which is a couple more than usual, but that's just something you must live with; so far so good. Then you realize four of those rooms are all under the same name and they are not blocked, or in other words, assigned a room number, so you must set up a room to match each of those four rooms. The other five arrivals already have a room assigned to them, so those you can get out of your mind for now. The four not assigned to a room are all under the same first and last name, for a guest who is the highest level in our loyalty program. It turns out he booked those four rooms into all king beds, but in the computer, we only have rooms with two queen size beds per room at this point in the night. To respect the guy's privacy, let's call him 'Mr. Johnson.' My coworker, who left a little after 11 p.m., didn't notice or care to set up the rooms for 'Mr. Johnson' because his reservations were made at 10:54 p.m. We do have a couple king beds left, but they are handicap accessible. And as experience shows, a loyalty member, at the highest level, would be dissatisfied with these rooms.

Kate listened intently trying to keep up with my scenario and asked, "So what will he say when he shows up?" *and* why do you think he needs *four* rooms?

"He had three other guys plus himself, which makes four. They're all businessmen visiting a local company. Of course, they booked it last minute, so as it turns out, I'm giving these guys the handicap rooms, plus a couple of double queens, and to add to the work load, I'm changing the names in our computer to match each person's actual name and updating their addresses by looking at their driver's licenses, plus searching for their membership number. Just so happens I had another couple of people behind them sitting and waiting on the couch in the lobby. Keep in mind I'm groggy, it's late. The guests probably have had a long, hard day. I don't mind updating information in the computer or searching for a loyalty number, that's easy stuff, but the *crux* of the matter is when the actual guy who booked the rooms, 'Mr. Johnson', comes up to the counter and sees I'm giving him the low floor handicap room. He doesn't know its handicap, but he knows it low floor because it begins with the number one. Right away he says, "Not first floor!" and that really pisses me off, but I can't get mad. It's my job to be polite. The problem is he doesn't realize that all I have is that first floor room, unless he wants a room with two queen beds.

"What's wrong with having the two queens?" Kate asked.

"You see, that's just it. There's nothing wrong with it for me or you, plus the queen size bed is more than large enough, but these guys are conditioned to wanting everything perfect. They stay at our hotel chain so many ridiculous number of times per year that they act like entitled hot shots or something. And basically, it's our job to treat them a little better than everyone else walking through the door, which I don't agree with, but what can I do about that?" I responded.

"OK, I'm with you so far," Kate said. So, what happened after he didn't like the first-floor room you tried to give him?"

"Well, I, being an honest man, let 'Mr. Johnson' know that when he booked his rooms, it was late, and we only had handicap rooms left with king size beds in them, plus the other couple of king bed rooms we had were not clean. They were empty, but they were not cleaned. So, believe it or not when he calls the 1-800 number to book the room, they give him a guaranteed reservation, not realizing the rooms are dirty. In other words, if the room is empty, then it's available for sale, dirty or clean, but nobody is going to clean rooms after midnight to prepare for a guest to arrive at any minute. The system doesn't make a whole lot of sense to me, but it's pretty much all about making money. It's the bottom line that matters in the hotel business, or at least at my hotel. Maybe a family run hotel or bed and breakfast operates differently to some degree. I bet sometimes they do and other times not but this much is true: it's frustrating as hell not getting respect from people like "Mr. Johnson" and it's hard to know what I'm going through unless you really experience it firsthand. The customer automatically assumes the blame goes to the person behind the counter and it's rare for them to ever put themselves in our shoes. A hotel has a limited number of rooms. You might have thirty-five or so clean spare rooms, ready to sell, on some nights at eleven p.m., but they are all rooms containing two queen beds, when what you happen to *need* are rooms with king beds. The customer doesn't know your availability and what's going on behind the scenes at the hotel, so he or she just walks in expecting to be treated like royalty or something.

Kate paused to digest what I had just said. Before she had a chance to say anything, I took a deep breath and said, "Is it all just complaining?" with a smile on my face.

"No, definitely not. It's *not* all just complaining," she said.

"Tell that to this guy Ryan."

"Who?"

"Oh, well don't worry about it. He's someone who was a 'hotel insider' and I actually reached out to him for some advice. But you know what I've come to realize Kate?"

"What?"

"I'm grateful for you. That's one. And two: a lot of people out there are just smoke and mirrors, kind of like this Ryan guy that I mentioned. He's like all perfect on the outside and comes across that way to most everyone. Some people can probably see right through him, if they don't like him for one reason or another. But I'm a nice guy and I guess I just think people like him are somewhat intimidating to me. You think of them as having all the answers but I'm having a lot of light bulb moments in my life lately. After meeting you, meeting Chen, just everything. Being a Christian now, it's like I'm realizing only God is the one who has all the answers and like Jesus said he's not a respecter of people. I think the idea is that people are people and don't make an idol out of them. Only God can judge us. Something like that. I think you just must show people respect without making one better than the other and do what you believe is right. And what I believe is right has got to line up with what God wants, right?"

"Well said," she looked at me attentively.

I stopped to think for a moment, glancing down.

"What is it Max?"

"I want to tell you something Kate."

"What is it?"

"I love you," I said.

She put her left hand on my shoulder and continued to focus her gaze on me. I knew, or at least I hoped I was correct, when I felt there was something special happening here.

"I love you too!" she said with excitement in her voice.

It's true I'm sentimental, but now I really felt something as my heart just melted in this moment. We happened to be still holding hands at the time; I could feel the warmth in her palm. As we got up to walk around some more and visit different stores, we got to know each other more thoroughly. Especially after I finally got a lot off my chest about work, she had the opportunity to talk more about herself. How she inherited her house after her grandparents passed away and all sorts of other stories.

We'd stopped here and there but knew the Connecticut shore was not something we'd conquer in one day, so it felt like time to get back on the road. What I loved was how we'd been lost in conversation on the ride back. It sure beats the ride back from the shore with one of my ex-girlfriends. In that ride back, we remained completely silent except for the sound of our breathing and the cars driving by. During that day, periodically my ex-girlfriend talked about this old guy friend she had known most of her life, a classmate. The guy probably never even spent any time with her outside of school, but she was infatuated with him it seemed. She'd never dated him but wanted to. Did the guy really like her? Why didn't he like her? I got to know a bit about this guy. But I just kept wondering. If you really like that guy, go track him down, ask him out or find someone else! I don't think of myself as the jealous type compared to the next guy, but my thinking is: don't waste my time. With Kate, it was different. She was into me. I'd shown her respect, a lot of respect. She appreciated that because she'd dated a so-called "bad boy" once before. She told me all about it earlier today. Kate didn't realize he was much of a bad boy in the first place. He'd gone along with her to church; he'd covered up his big tattoos (they were not visible unless shirtless) and when his anger became apparent, he smashed a coffee mug on the floor one day finally, proceeded to take off his shirt, revealing the big tattoos, which she did not know about, and on a separate occasion tried to force her into bed, which she was able to avoid completely by yelling at him which happened to cause him to stop harassing her. That was the last she'd seen of him. It was good information she'd shared with me. I wanted to know her more and I was happy she'd wanted to know every detail about me, something I didn't get from past girlfriends. Back to our car ride at present. We'd continued our conversation and because it was so all encompassing, we'd missed the proper exit back to her home, so I'd thought of a solution.

"Are you up for a stop at Connecticut's finest mall?" I offered.

"Sure Max, I can spend time with you at Connecticut's worst mall. Heck, I can spend time with you at Rhode Island's worst mall," she added.

So, with that I pulled into the parking lot of Westfarms Mall. I'd explained to her that the mall was actually situated in both West Hartford and Farmington. Newington was right on this road as well as New Britain. "It's a little confusing so don't quote me on that!" I let her know. Across the street from us, back in the 1990's, they had an actual Coconuts store selling music, movies, stuff like that. I guess you appreciate it more when it's gone. Times will never be the same. Where do you find places like that now? Similar stores, yeah, they are rare though. Very rare. Joe's American Bar and Grill, the place was incredible. Also located across the street fifteen years ago. Just a piece of Connecticut nostalgia, gone forever.

"Or, how about going to Blockbuster

Video on a date and renting a movie together, as a couple?" she emphasized the words as a couple.

I thought it was cute. "What about a local, *family run* video store? I can remember some going waaaay back," I said.

We walked while we talked from the car to the main entrance. She said "Wait," holding one hand signaling me to stop, then walked in front of me and held the door open for me with a laugh. Now I know she really had to love me to hold the door open for me, even if it was just a joke. At least she cared. Really cared. I could just tell. Again, let's hope it lasts.

We passed through the mall, walking casually. "You see this corner here? That was once the site of the Thomas Kinkade Galleries, you know, 'The Painter of Light.' I was shocked at the high prices of the paintings back in the late 90s. After asking more questions and learning they were mere reproductions only, not original paintings. But to be fair, not just any reproductions. Artists were hired to add special touches with real paint, highlighting the works. Say what you want about the man's work, because I know there were oh so many opinions about it; I really loved what he did. The paintings lit up the room with the technique he used. I got this book about Thomas' life from the library which was sort of an exposé but really eye opening," I told her.

She was walking behind me off to my right and suddenly snuck up right beside my shoulder and pressed up against me. It felt nice to know her signs of affection were so immediate. Once again, I felt God was answering my prayers. This time she directly reached for my hand and interlocked our fingers.

"Let's get a coffee *here*," I said.

"I'm paying, Ohhkay? She said pulling out her wallet.

I liked the way she said OK, sort of different every time but her voice was just perfect. Did I like it better than her look? Probably about the same. We both got two small French roasts, milk, no sugar. She said she was copying me. I was OK with that. With my first couple of sips, I realized the temperature was just right. The flavor? Impeccable. And the coffee shop? Well, I didn't think they actually *had* one like this left here. I was under the impression major chains were all that were left. Little did I know AJ's Coffee was here in existence.

I talked to her about the mall stores which were once in business here. She really didn't know about them because she didn't get out to places like this so much years ago, as I did. There were rectangular fountains spread out all around here on the ground level. They were very cool. The lights were gentle, and the water was bubbling up just a little. I could still smell it now in my memory. A unique scent. Not like a swimming pool exactly. Countless coins resting at the bottom.

"Long gone are the days of Dalton Books, FAO Swartz, The Sharper Image, Software Etc., and the list goes on. At this mall anyways. I can tell you this much; I'll never forget the days of youth walking around here with my cousin. We'd always grab a sample of the iced mocha drink but never actually buy one. Maybe we were just brought up to be cheap to some degree. Three dollars something for a drink back in 1992 was a lot of money, for a kid anyways. And those cool Oakley sunglasses were at least one hundred dollars, so we'd dream about buying them one day. Nevertheless, we had a lot of fun," I said.

"So, did you like the veggie burger you got at the outlets today?" she asked.

"Yes, veggie burger, lettuce, tomato, pickle, mayo, fries and ketchup on the side with a Coke. It's like an experiment. See what it's like to be vegetarian, not with a fancy exotic dish but just burger and fries. See if it's available and where. Chen tells me Larry's daughter is vegetarian," I said.

"Larry's daughter?"

"Yeah."

"Why do you care about Larry's daughter?" she asked.

"I don't even know what she looks like. I gather Chen was interested in her," I said.

"The Center, Larry, all this, it's an obsession for you, isn't it?" she said.

"I don't know. I know that I go deeply into things when I am interested in them. I tried to get his book. The larger hardcover one which is semi auto-biographical but also self-help, I suppose. It's fifty-two bucks used online, out of print, that's why. Chen has his other book, the shorter glossy paperback, 'wild and wacky' full of pictures and so forth. He's been meaning to give me it, but I really need to get my hands on it," I said.

"I'm not sure what to think of this Max," she said.

"You know, I was in Florida not that long ago visiting my parents, brother, etc. It was my first time in Clearwater, so I'd taken in all the sights, including the Scientology buildings. I'd had nothing on the agenda that day, so I'd asked if some family members with me would like to take a tour. It was one of Scientology's most important locations. They said no, very adamantly, and gave a couple reasons why. But to me it was a wasted opportunity because when would I be back to Clearwater? You see, I go deeply into things I get interested in, even though I wasn't looking to join The Church of Scientology, I just wanted to experience the tour, see the design of the building from the inside, first hand. Maybe even take a communications course. And it's like that with The Center, Larry's Center. Although it's different in the sense that it's not a church or a temple.

"I respect what you're saying Max, but, be careful. Before we head home for the night. Let's stop at that nice park next to the mall and take a little walk, then pray on the bench," she said.

"I think that's a good idea," I responded.

While the night came to a close, I dropped Kate off at her house. I felt pretty beat from a long day, but I felt it in a good way. When my head would hit the pillow, I was going to appreciate a good night's rest. Something that I never *could* appreciate much when working the night shift, apart from my two nights off per week, which really just served as a tease. The fact that Kate and I were not sleeping in the same bed was a *good* thing. We'd not had to go into it beyond a few words in conversation. Both of us were on the same page. Years ago, I thought differently; I acted differently. But, I wasn't really a Christian then. Even if I was, would I have given in to temptation had I'd been dating someone without a faith and discipline as strong as Kate's? You see, cousins of mine, even immediate family, perhaps Chen as well, they'd all question why I'd not sleep with Kate, no doubt. It's pretty simple really. Lying in bed, alone, is not so bad when you have hope you'll marry her one day. In fact, the honeymoon wouldn't be so great If I'd slept with her before marriage. We'd just be a couple of hypocrites and we want *more* than that out of life.

Chapter 14

A Night to Remember

I had gotten a call from Chen, earlier in the day. "What are you doing Max? Would you like to come with me, over to my friend Luke's place?" he asked. Catching me off guard, I made a quick decision saying, "Why not," not really knowing who this Luke character was. Someone else could enter the picture and also become a friend of mine. Michael Chen was one in a million as far as his personality went, so I wasn't quite sure who'd be similar to him anyways, but I was kind of an odd bird myself. Or so I've been called this once before.

I decided to head over to the local gym and purchase a pass for ten dollars. I needed to blow off some steam and get the blood flowing. I did a whole 5k on the treadmill. I'm paying for the day pass; I might as well make it worthwhile. I later did a routine with two to three sets of exercises for each basic muscle group. Two sets of shoulder press, three sets of bench press to stimulate the chest and triceps, three sets of alternating bicep curls using the dumb bells and so on. I even stopped to use the sauna afterwards. The man sitting nearby said, "I come in here once in a while, just to warm up my bones." I didn't know they even had a sauna. It kind of makes me consider joining this gym in the future. I continued to eagerly await another call from Chen giving me further details, "sometime around five I'll hit you up," he said earlier.

As I was leaving the parking lot of the gym I threw a CD into my car stereo. Pat McGee Band: "Revel," It sounded remarkably close to the Dave Matthews Band but in some hard to explain way, a little different. They were both from Virginia after all. Saxophone and drums both being played in a unique way. I heard my phone ring and decided to answer it using the speaker phone option. "Hi, this is Max."

"I'm going to give you some directions Max; do you know New Britain at all?" And on Chen went describing to me where his friend Luke's apartment was. "Meet us there in an hour." I got showered and threw on a button-down shirt, a Van Heusen. A combination of subtle colors, but an overriding greenish hue along with a pair of khakis and brown boots, and then I splashed on some Aspen Cologne just for a bit of nostalgia from my high school days. I didn't even know whether you could buy this scent in stores anymore, I got it online, Ebay. Just the bottle alone with its forest green color and gold cap, etched leaf as a symbol, made me happy. I had no time to waste so I just headed on over. When I knocked on the door a man around my age greeted me. "Hi, you must be Max. I'm Luke Daniel Caprio, aka L-D-C."

I stepped inside the place and surveyed the scene. A relatively clean and neat apartment. A poster on the wall, framed. Beers of the World. With many bottles from various countries. I wanted to break the ice. "I like that, 'Beers of the World,'" Always wanted one of those pictures.

"Maahhxy! What's new buddy?" Chen shouted out with excitement.

"Nothing really, I got a good workout in." I noticed they'd started on the beers and had a couple on the coffee table. An electronic dance song was playing in the background- distinctively European sounding-at a comfortable level of volume.

"Can I have a beer?" I was wasting no time.

"One brewski coming up," Luke replied. I sat down on an arm chair in the center of the room over by Chen while Luke got up to grab me a cold one from the fridge. He sat back down next to Chen on the couch. I took a long refreshing sip, more of a gulp really. Something about a beer after a workout makes it that much better. I reached for a handful of almonds I saw on the table. Tortilla chips and salsa in two separate bowls were also there.

"How did you guys become friends?" I asked.

"I met Chen back in high school. But, people usually called him Mike. I was the one who really coined the name Chen as a nickname," Luke Replied.

"I don't know that he 'coined' the nickname, but I know that suddenly people were just calling me "Chen", it was like "Chen, Chen, Chen" all the time people saw me. I was OK with it too," he got up and walked over to the kitchen placing his beer on the counter, next he went for another one. "LDC here, 'Luke', just has been a good friend over the years and we've basically always kept in touch, which is not always the case this many years after high school.

The conversation went on and I soon realized Luke Daniel Caprio was a walking encyclopedia of sports knowledge. He'd given us so many stats from major league baseball then went onto boxing. Coincidentally the three of us all happened to be major fans of Mike Tyson.

"Boxing was way more fun in the 90s and 80s for that matter Max," Luke said. "Someone like Tyson did amazing things for the sport. He was such a dynamic character, in and out of the ring, with his lavish lifestyle. And when he finally lost for the first time to James "Buster" Douglas in Japan-think about it-do people really make a big deal now, the way they did then, when a champ loses his belt?" he continued. Luke was kind of like a hyperactive motor mouth, but I liked the guy so far.

"You know, there is something special about boxing from that era. Maybe it's just that we are nostalgic about it because it brings us back to when we were kids or teens? I don't know? Did you ever see that movie, 'Great White Hype'? It's a comedy," I said.

"Oh yeah, that was great, with Jeff Goldblum" Luke responded.

"Or, what's that other one in Atlantic City? With Nick Cage?" I asked.

"Oh, I know, something about dice, right? What's it called?" Chen responded.

"Snake Eyes!" Luke Shouted out. "A sexy, fast-paced thriller! Wooohooo!"

The mood was fun here and I was taking a liking to it. I found myself going back in time and remembering simpler, more carefree days like when I was in my late teens and earlier twenties. I had lost touch with friends I'd had, guys sort of like these two, but remarkably things were changing in my life so rapidly now. It was almost as if removing my job, temporarily at that, was the solution or magic bullet to the despair I felt stuck at that miserable hotel. The other part of me also felt that God was answering my prayers with all the pleasant excitement in my life, especially the addition of a girlfriend namely Kate whom was just perfect in my mind. I sat back and sunk into the soft chair to enjoy the moment while it lasted.

"So, are you a member of the Center Luke?" I asked.

"What center?" he responded.

"Oh, well the uh Larry Espenschied Center, LEC, Chen is really big into it, so I thought maybe you were a part of it too," I followed up.

"Nope, but I'd be up for checking it out sometime."

Chen took his empty beer bottle and tossed it vertically in the air about the distance of a foot and caught it with his right hand squeezing the bottle while his muscles flexed.

"Nice biceps, Chenny!" Luke joked.

"Yeah, you *are* super fit man," I added.

Chen got up with a serious expression on his face. He walked in front of the coffee table and spun around facing the kitchen, back towards us, threw up both of his arms in the air and gave a real muscleman pose. Then he turned around and took off his shirt like a professional wrestler and proceeded to flex in all the classic pro body builder poses. Both Luke and I laughed but clearly, we were impressed.

"Look at those abs," Luke remarked.

"And the chest, you can see all the striations. You're chiseled man," I said.

The sound of a text message came next. Chen reached for his pocket, carefully looking at his phone.

"Party tonight guys."

"Where?" both Luke and I responded at about the same time.

"Litchfield."

"Litchfield? Really? I love Litchfield," I said.

"Yeah, out on West Street."

We'd all agreed on going to the party and Luke was nice enough to drive. We all hopped in his car and headed west. Although the drive was a little long, it was pleasant through the Litchfield Hills. On the left was a sign for a stop on the Connecticut Wine Trail, further down the road, Our Lady of Lourdes Shrine in Litchfield, where they had a regular tag sale and outdoor walking along the stations of the cross. An actual piece of stone directly from the Lourdes site in France was a part of the grotto. Then we drove up the hill and stopped at a house along the right-hand side of West Street. There was something so different about this area that had always stood out for me since I'd first visited it as a kid one Saturday. Much different from a lot of towns in central Connecticut. There was a small town, rural charm to it. You had everything you really needed here and the old-fashioned homes along this hill were always appealing to me.

We got out of the car and jogged up to the front door. "Come on in!" Rick was a member of the Center, I later learned, and somewhat of a friend to Chen. The house was a simple but beautiful early 1900's house. Hardwood floors throughout and as I walked on through the place, I realized this was the first time I'd actually been inside of someone's *home* in Litchfield, which was a much different experience than all the businesses or museums I visited. Taking a leisurely drive out here so often in the past for me was just a way to get away from it all, but I'd stop at the coffee shop to read for a while, then the coffee shop closed down for good. On future visits I'd stop at the café inside of a sit-down restaurant to get my coffee to go. Later a burrito at the Mexican restaurant and then I'd continue my journey. Little things like that made me so happy until eventually I'd explored every nook and cranny of the town, so it seemed, and I'd then move onto another part of Connecticut for a while to relieve my boredom.

"Do you like Old Speckled Hen beer Max? Try this," Rick said while handing me a bottle. He was the owner of the home.

"I'd like to try it, thank you," I responded.

I'd wondered about Rick, Larry, who hadn't been here, but led the Center, Chen, the whole bunch of folks connected to all this really. Not in a bad way but in a curious excited kind of way. Where did I fit in? I'd loved the Center, Larry's Center out in Warren. It isn't all that far from here. Did Rick personally know Larry? Is that how he got hooked up with the Center or did he just join the Center and then become friends with Larry or did he not know

Larry personally? I felt Chen was on the cusp of something big in life. He'd wanted out of his career in insurance. Badly. I'd wanted out of the hotel business and maybe there'd be an opportunity for me in Larry's world as well. I get the feeling Larry is rich. After all, I'd become friends with Chen so quickly and felt drawn to the work they were doing. Did it really conflict with my Christian beliefs? Still, Chen had hit somewhat of a dead end in life and Larry was maybe his immediate opportunity for real change. Where else was he to turn? Financially in trouble after helping his dishonest ex-girlfriend, living under his parents roof again as a result of the money he gave her and never got back. I, on the other hand, had, at one point at least, a great teaching position at a private academy and a degree from Lake Ontario Beach University. With Kate in my life I'd have an opportunity to unlock new doors in the future, both career wise and otherwise socially. I still felt somewhat of a tug of war going on inside me, but in time I'd see where my life would head. *Soon*, hopefully.

"What kind of music do you want to hear?!" Rick yelled out from up top of the stairs. By this point I'd grabbed my second beer and found the Old Speckled hen to be quite possibly the best tasting beer I'd ever had. Who was I kidding? There was no better beer I could think of offhand. Sam Adam's Boston Lager? Boston ale? The cream ale was good, they were all good but the Speckled Hen, this was even better.

"Los Lonely Boys" I yelled out, so he could clearly hear me. I stood next to Chen. His friend Luke Daniel Caprio had wandered somewhere.

"Los what? Los Who?" Rick yelled out.

"LOS LONELY BOYS!!" Chen and I simultaneously blurted out.

"Oh, Yes, I think I've got it," Rick made his exit down the hallway.

Chen and I continued conversation. I'd had to say I was having one of the best nights I'd had in a long time. Well, there'd been a lot of good nights and days lately, especially with Kate, but this, this was different in the sense that it brought me back to my somewhat younger days in that here I was at a fun and spirited house party in this old farmhouse, just having a blast. And suddenly I hear Los Lonely Boys playing on the stereo. Electric guitar strumming like there was no tomorrow.

"High five!" Luke had come out of nowhere, his hand positioned high up in the air. Smack! I hit him with a high five and he joined our conversation. At one point the three of us started laughing uncontrollably. A couple of fine looking older ladies found the laughing to be contagious and joined in. It took a while for us all to settle down.

The night went on for a few hours more and at one-point Rick asked us about who was driving home and where we were heading? "You guys are staying here if you'd like. I have a spare bedroom on the top floor with two beds. There's also a couch. You can wrestle over who gets to sleep where if you'd like but I just don't want you guys driving home drunk. It worked out well for me because by the time we would have gotten back to New Britain I'd have to be sobered up and drive home which was risky, so why not just stay here. "Coffee and breakfast in the morning fellas," Rick said as he patted us on the back.

I'd realized nights like this were the type which made things all right in life. They made sense out of things. On the one hand it's true you don't accomplish a whole lot standing around and drinking at a party but on the other hand that sense of comradery, friendship and just plain fitting in left a lasting impression on me. And it was fun. A lot of fun. You look back later with a sense of wonder and awe about nights like this. I learned about Chen some more. His life has been essentially the good and the bad. Ups and downs. Sure, there was the bullying. Not fitting in with the crowd. I myself could relate to that to some degree. I'd joke with Chen about who had the more dysfunctional family but after a while I realized that Chen's family was more dysfunctional. In my case my brother moved down to Florida when offered a good job opportunity along with the wife. My parents followed down after him a year later. I was happily here in Connecticut with most of my other relatives in nearby towns. Chen had learned some important lessons in life by this time. He'd reminisced telling me stories back to when he'd been on his final year in high school. He'd become radically different looking because of his work done at the dermatologist and with his weight loss but it didn't solve all his problems. It's a good lesson. Great lesson. This is what he told me. But this is also my own interpretation of what he told me. Chen got recognition from his fellow classmates for his new look. Girls, he said were interested in him that would have never been interested in him a year prior. Of course, he lost some of those chances with the girls who were all of a sudden interested in him, but he took other chances that he was comfortable with. A date with someone he'd met while playing pool out on the Berlin Turnpike, for instance. Sure, the girl lived practically on the other side of Connecticut, but he'd do what he could to try to make it work. But the reason why all his problems were not really fixed was because he'd been fighting in his head against other people's opinions of him. Like poignantly demonstrated one day when a friend of Chen's was playing basketball with them in the driveway. Whether it was competitiveness over the simple game of one-on-one or just some kind of undetermined threat this friend of a friend felt. But words got exchanged and tempers flared. He'd said to Chen that he'd known about him and what a real loser he was with no friends in school. For Chen, who had told me this story during our conversations, it was crushing. This kid was a student at another school, a private school, but knew people from Chen's school. Chen wondered why things just couldn't be different for him. Here was a kid who could have been a friend but just remained an acquaintance and now a mean spirited one at that. The reality I knew from my own philosophy on life was that things took time to take effect in life. It's like the Christian parable of the sowing and reaping. Chen's past had effects or ramifications that wouldn't all together go away. The new changes in life he was making or made already had positive effects also, but things cannot just magically all become perfect instantly. Of course, the frustration is that when you want to resolve something, and it just is not resolving itself, you can fight it, fight it, and fight it some more but, in the end, maybe it's time to look at things differently. Fighting against someone else's opinion of you: Could you not take their opinion and determine it to be true? What if you don't want to face the truth? You keep fighting against it. But what if you accept the truth and find a positive perspective in it? Then realize not everyone's opinion is the truth but sometimes it is. Not everyone will tell you everything they feel either. They'll tell you what they are comfortable telling you at that moment. And when push comes to shove, they'll tell you more sometimes.

We're not all the same. Why is it hard for a unique or non-typical person to accept their uniqueness? Do people want to be called weird? One in a million? Strange? Bizarre? Where does each person draw the line and how does each person process how they see themselves? We've all been through many different things in life. Some harder than others but often it seems many people end up feeling insecure-whether they show it or not, but should they feel insecure? Do they have to? For how long?

Chapter 15

Chen's Finest Hour

"Hello, this is Michael," He said answering his phone.

"Chen, it's me, Max," I responded sitting in my car in the plaza of a coffee shop I'd found for the first time today, phone to my ear.

"What's new my friend? How's your day going so far?"

"Well actually I ordinarily wouldn't call you during the day since you might be busy working and all, sitting at a comfortable chair in a tall office building in the capital city, but…" I started to say.

"You got me at a good time. I am taking an early break and I've still got some more time to spare."

"OK good. Can you believe it? I'm all the way out here in New York state. I got so bored with everything in Connecticut that I wanted to get inspired by something new. Plus, I was up so early since I've been messing around with my sleep routine lately. One day we're out drinking and the next I'm crashing early. I was sitting at this coffee shop on a soft couch in the corner by a window just reading and watching everything around me. It felt good to be free and get away from it all. I could be back home in about an hour and a half. Are you free after work? We can take a drive to a Starbucks or maybe have dinner?" I asked.

"Tonight, well actually uhhh…"

I could sense he'd had something on his mind, but I just didn't know what yet. Maybe something he didn't want me to know. "Do you have plans?"

"Actually, I'm really a little nervous about it, but also really, really excited too. It's completely an impromptu thing Max. I would have told you about it otherwise. I've been asked by top dog himself, Larry; he wants me to make a speech, a presentation, in front of all the Center. It's a talk about health and weight loss. You know, eating, lifestyle. A bit of my own personal story sprinkled in. He's given me free range to say what I want so long as I cover certain topics such as nutrition. An example of what to eat for improved health and more practical things since we have an audience at the Center who want to hear some solid practical advice," he said.

"That's great Chen, Congratulations!"

"It's the first major, major thing I've done at the Center in this capacity and I think it's going to solidify a spot for me to get a room there, like live and work. Actually, move into the Center. I can get out of my temporary living arrangements with the parents, hopefully get to work with Larry and get paid, then put an end to my desk job at the insurance company, I hope. Key word hope," he explained.

"Just tell me when and I'm there. I'll take the ride out to Warren. We can even ride together," I offered.

"Well that's the thing Max, you know you did attend with me for that seminar where we talked all day and you got to see the Center."

"Yeah and I loved it."

"But that was a free event"

"So, what's the cost?"

"There's no cost per event most of the time Max; it's a yearly membership fee and when you have that pretty much everything becomes free. All the talks, all the seminars, the gym, sure donations are accepted here and there but once you're in the Center, you're in the center. As for me, I don't pay anymore because I work so closely with Larry. He considers me a part of the team."

"What's the cost?"

"$700 dollars per year Max, but that offers you a lot. Say, the time we were there that day, you got a lot of out of it. Just think what you'll get with unlimited visits for a year. And you know there is the exercise facility and café also. Of course, there's those mysterious rooms that I don't even know about!" Chen explained.

"I see, well seven hundred dollars is a little steep, but I feel it's worth it and I don't want to miss out on you speaking tonight, so long as I have a choice to opt out of membership in one year."

"Nobody leaves Max, once you're in you're in."

I paused for a moment to let that sink in. "Seriously? Because I don't really think that…"

"Max, I'm joking. I have to be there in advance, so please, I'd love to have you there, please just if you can drive on your own because I have many things to go over personally with Mr. Espenschied beforehand, but also don't forget to leave early enough so you can sign up with your membership in the gift shop. That's where it's done. Remember, allow an extra half an hour. Oh, and it starts at 6:00 p.m., on the main stage. You need to wear at tuxedo. See you then.

"A tux?"

"I'm only joking about the tux."

"OK looking forward to it buddy," I hung up and sat in my car. $700? What was I getting myself into? It was reasonable, wasn't it?

I headed home from New York state by taking I-84 east and was able to beat the traffic as it was early enough in the day. I guess I was kind of on a high by feeling inspired seeing new spots out west and even walking by the Hudson River. When I got home although I did feel relieved to be done with all that driving. I lit a cinnamon candle once I got into the bathroom. One of those large ones with three wicks. I took in a deep breath and ran the water in the tub. I'd take a bubble bath to relax and kill some time. I poured a milk and honey scented bubble bath under the hot water. I thought about Kate and looked forward to Chen's speech tonight. I'd decided to bring a notebook and pen to jot down key points of his talk. I rested my head on the bath pillow and took another long breath. The hot water soothed my body and helped to circulate my blood flow. After my bath, I got dressed but felt I could no longer sit around the house anymore. I put on a pair of khakis and a red checkered shirt layered with navy and green colors as well. I sprayed on some CK Obsession cologne and got in the car. I decided

I'd walk out at the White Memorial Conservation Center in Bantam, as I'd have so much spare time. It felt good to walk out whatever frustrations I was feeling today.

I'd arrived at the center early enough to admire all the architectural details I loved so much my first time here. I swooped into the gift shop which itself was a work of art to me anyways. I'd not gotten a chance to browse all through it last time. The postcards, a book with photos of the center and member testimonials. In fact, I didn't know this such book existed. When I asked about books authored by Lawrence Espenschied, none were available. I suppose what I saw on the internet was true, one book out of print and used copies priced super high. Someday I'd find a copy. Then the other so called by Chen, "wacky and wonderful" book is out there, but he'd misplaced his copy. 'I'm sure it's up there on the shelf somewhere, next time Max," he'd said. Was he trying to hide something from me about Lawrence? Perhaps his ex-girlfriend borrowed his copy and never got the chance to return it? Or it's all just my overactive imagination?

Stuffed animals and teddy bears, magnets, coffee mugs and the like were all neatly displayed for sale. Not that much was specific to the Center. Almost none of it labeled the "Lawrence Espenschied Center," LEC, or anything of the like. Merely fun items. Positive quotes galore and all types of things for sale. Candles, mixed nuts, ground coffee even. Next, I was looking for shot glasses but to no avail. I'd approached the woman behind the counter, her name badge read Bridgette. She looked to be about in her late twenties with bright blonde hair which was straight and parted down the middle. I couldn't help but notice she also happened to have a large bust. She was heavy set and wore a bright, sky-blue polo shirt. "I would like to sign up for a membership. I was told it's necessary to do so in order to attend tonight's speech?" I said.

"Yes, I'd be happy to help you with that," she said, tapping her fingers on the counter. The color of her finger nails was painted to match her sky-blue shirt. I looked at her and noticed her sparkling blue eyes which seemed to color coordinate with her whole appearance. She also had rather chubby cheeks and looked beautiful when she smiled. "Please come with me and I'll have you fill out an application."

She began to lead me through a door behind her off to her left. She had on khaki pants and had a curvy, round figure. This was exciting I thought. We went through a short hallway. I could see an office through the window in the door to my left and yet another off to my right. Then we sat in a room at the end of the hallway. She flipped on the light and I sat in a teal colored chair along with a large plant to my right in the corner of the room. I looked up, down, left, right and again was impressed with all the little details that went along with this place. I suppose it's good I left the house so early as the application was a solid three pages long.

"Please follow me," she said as she took the application from my hand.

Earlier I said this was the final room at the end of the hallway but in fact I was wrong. She pressed a button on the wall and another door opened which led us to yet another final room. In there I waited while I listened to some light instrumental music. It was your typical office room. The chair was remarkably comfortable and on the coffee table in front of me was the hardcover book showcasing the Center.

"Would you like a coffee, tea while you wait?"

What the hell I thought, why not. "Sure, I'll have a coffee, milk no sugar please, that'd be great."

"This shouldn't take long," she responded. In less than ten minutes she'd returned.

"Right this way," she said with a smile in her voice.

We walked back to the gift shop and I paid her in full while she printed a receipt and took my photo for the membership ID.

"You can wear this around your neck if you'd like; just scan it when you go in anywhere it's required. Welcome to the Larry Espenschied Center, Enjoy!"

"Thanks Bridgette," I responded.

I had a feeling of nervous excitement, kind of like Chen was speaking of earlier. I was happy, and now I was about to go listen to my friend speak. I passed through the main auditorium and had my badge scanned, took a seat and leaned forward in eager anticipation. Soft music played in the background; the chatter of at least a hundred guests bounced around the room.

"Ladies and Gentlemen, Can I have your attention please?" Mr. Lawrence Espenschied himself front and center stage announced as the crowd quickly quieted down. "We're pleased to have a special speaker for you tonight. Many of you know him already. He's been a member here for several years now, but his journey goes back years before that. He'd discovered my work and put it into use. The beauty of what I set out to do has been seen in the fruits of many of your labors here in the audience and our speaker is yet another fine example of that. What I'm speaking about, more specifically, is how my work sometimes being more general so that you can decide how you'd like to use it in your own life results in unique accomplishments. In other words, rather than me telling you specifically how to live. 'Do this, do that, don't do this, avoid this specific thing,' No, that's not what I set out to do but rather help you to become a truer version of yourself. Your real self. And one of the ways our speaker tonight has done this is through his personal journey of weight loss and health. He's been working on a cookbook that I can't talk much about just yet, however, it may just be in our very own gift shop one day. But he has much, much more to talk with you about than just that so without further ado I introduce you to Mr.

Michael Chen." A thunderous applause came over the auditorium for several seconds then rippled out gently.

"Thank you, thank you, thank you *very* much. I'm Michael Chen. It's a beautiful Connecticut spring evening here in Litchfield County. I once was speaking to a former girlfriend of mine, several years ago. This is a true story. I had been determined to regain my ideal weight because I'll admit I got into a slump. I had gained some weight but was within fifteen pounds of where I needed to be. She was rather heavy but that was not of concern to me. I just point it out to you because it pertains to the story. I'd said to her something in conversation along the lines of achieving an ideal body. Now, I can't remember the context precisely, but I wasn't speaking about her, that's for sure. I was just speaking about achieving an ideal body. Now her response was: 'there is no ideal body, ideal face etc.' Now there is where I believe she was wrong, and I'd like to explain to you what I mean by that. And you can disagree or agree with me but first, allow me to explain. The ideal body is connected to the ideal weight, you can use those terms interchangeably in this case. I had a goal to lose that fifteen pounds I mentioned earlier and by doing so I'd be at my ideal weight, so I think we can all agree on that. Now, by reaching that ideal weight I'd be at my ideal body. Now, that does not mean perfect. There is no perfect, for instance my height is only so tall, I'm not a tall guy and I'm not especially short either. But to me, by reaching that ideal weight, I'd achieved my ideal body. You see what my ex-girlfriend was doing was equating the ideal body and the ideal face saying you can't achieve it so just accept yourself the way you are. In other words, give up! But you see, you can make the argument that she's half right because your face is your face. She was confusing the issue. You look a certain way and let's say a person is not particularly nice looking then they can't achieve that ideal face unless they wanted to go to a fancy plastic surgeon, but I don't agree with that and that proves the point also that you can't do it on your own. But you see the body is *different*, you can achieve that ideal weight which in turn automatically gives you the ideal body. What is in our control? And what is outside of your control? Now, I mention this story to make the point that some people do not believe in themselves when it comes to certain things. My ex-girlfriend did not believe that she could lose x number of pounds and be at a healthy, normal weight. She was under the limited belief that she'd be heavy all her life.

That's not to say that she'd be more or less attractive this way or that way, but this is a psychological matter having to do with what you believe is true and possible. And we can pick this topic apart even more and look at it from different angles. Beauty is in the eye of the beholder let's say. In that case you may already have the ideal face to someone but to so many others you don't but that's a different point entirely. I'm here tonight in this brief talk to let you know what you can do to improve your life measurably."

I leaned back into my seat and enjoyed listening to Chen's talk. I glanced down at my watch, then looked around the room stretching my arms and back using the arm rests on the chair for support. A couple exchanged a few words speaking quietly into each other's ears as not to disturb the speech. I looked further back into the audience; Bridgette, who'd sold me the membership earlier, was looking straight ahead attentively. I noticed she was most likely alone and not with a date or anything. I studied her for a few seconds, loosing track of what Chen was saying. She made eye contact with me and smiled, chubby cheeks. So cute. Hmmm, I thought, maybe she's thinking I like her or she might like me, or she just could be happy she'd signed me up considering there probably had to have been some incentive waiting for her like a one percent commission or something of the such. I don't know, at least they'd notice she'd sign me up, Larry would notice most likely. Or was she curious about me. She'd have all my info from those applications and she'd likely do a Google search wondering about my life. She'd be able to see I was in a relationship on Facebook for instance. Or maybe none of it mattered at all to her. Either way I was happy to be here and if Kate had anything negative to say about it I'd have a good excuse for signing up: 1) I'd have to get a membership to hear Chen speak and he was my best friend. I just couldn't miss it. 2) Similar to point number one, because Chen was my new best friend and he'd had a membership here -for so many years- it'd be my opportunity to spend time with him and see what it was all about at this place. 3) the center had exercise facilities and what's more important than exercise? Plus, I'd have the best trainer to work with, Mr. Chen himself. I could go on like this but ultimately, for me personally I was just plain drawn to the Center itself. Where else do you see such an eclectic blend of architectural genius? Well, yes, you do see great contemporary architecture around Connecticut here and there but maybe it's the place you work, and you hate your job or maybe it's a college or house, but what good does that do to you if you don't go to school there or live there. But here, here was a center that you could actually belong to and there was a café you could eat at, shoot the breeze, sip a coffee. And then there was that gift shop. I love gift shops, perhaps it all began on field trips back in grade school or trips to Florida and the ubiquitous Florida gift shops selling everything from orange flavored chocolate to shot glasses which had messages written on them like 'I got squeezed in Florida.' And the Center's gift shop gave me that feeling all over again. It was not just a rinky-dink gift shop, no, it had a plethora of items in it. It made you feel like you can come back each week and buy something new for yourself. Ah ha, I got it. I can even buy Kate a gift like that stuffed toy dolphin I saw earlier.

Chen continued speaking, "Fiber, Fiber is so important. In one large apple there are five grams of fiber. He held up his hand stretching out his fingers, indicating the number of grams, one per finger, five in total. In one cup of lentils there are sixteen grams of fiber. SIX-TEEN G-R-A-H-M-S" he slowly enunciated his words so that nobody would be mistaken. On he went speaking of the importance of fiber and how it worked in the body. "Some of you may be vegetarians or vegans. You may be flexitarians or semi-vegetarians. You may be considering it for the future. This next bit is for you. Whatever the case may be, you need to stop and think about your diet. Examine how you're living. How are you eating? Think about your fellow meat eaters and think about whether or not they eat so many bagels, pizzas or pastas. This is not to say avoid these types of foods because, let me tell you, I truly love these foods, but you have to put them into their proper proportion. When or if you cut meat out you need to fill that void with something. How are you going to fill it? Think variety too. On and on he went while the audience remained quiet and attentive. I can say that I'd learned a thing or two, but more so I was impressed with Chen's seemingly comfortable mastery of public speaking. Larry also had the field of public speaking in his toolbelt of skills. Larry was also goofy at times. He'd be one part serious and one part goofy which was good because by being goofy you are sort of demonstrating to the world- *Hey, I'm not perfect, there is no perfect, I'm me.*

"I'd like to give a shout out to my good friend Max. Max, I know you're out there, yes, there you are, I see you. Max is a new member to our group and I'm really pleased he could join us today. I think he's going to want to discuss my speech with me later. Ironing out the details of everything I've said. He's a philosopher and that is what he does but that's why I get along with him so well. He thinks and then when he's done thinking he thinks some more. And when he speaks, well, he likes to hear his own voice." I could hear some laughing in the audience. "I believe this is what it means to have a degree in philosophy. We all needed a bit of comic relief at this point in the conversation. Right? I once had Max explain to me Aristotle. But it was a good thing I'd ordered an extra shot of espresso that day. If he put his talks on audio book, there'd be a good alternative to sleeping pills....No, I'm only kidding. Max is really a good guy and his own simple straight-forward modern-day philosophy is what you're going to love if you ever get the opportunity to meet him."

On my way out of the auditorium, I swung by the gift shop. I'd buy that toy dolphin for Kate after all plus throw in a chocolate bar with almonds, along with a pack of gum for myself. It felt good to be here tonight. I wondered about how many members belonged

to this organization. What were *their* stories?
Where did I fit in? Would I ever fit in *anywhere*
really? I knew I'd liked what I saw and where I
was for now. I'd just take it one day at a time.

Chapter 16

Things are Going Wrong

Kate and I had tentative plans for the weekend coming up, Friday maybe. Nothing set in stone. It was on my mind, but I didn't want to smother her, so I thought I would lay off for a bit. I had given the cousins, Robert and Sally, a break, or had they given me a break? It was OK, I felt the timing was right with all the new excitement in my life; maybe it was for the best.

I went about my regular routine. Chen had gotten me more motivated to keep up with an exercise regimen, so I did my regular neighborhood walk and when I got back in the house, I showered, made a breakfast wrap for myself along with a half glass of orange juice and a second cup of coffee. I was ready to take a drive in no particular direction. I'd become tired of the same dull routine in terms of my usual coffee shops. The library was just not enticing enough either at this point because I needed to see the goings-on rather than just feel secluded in a library. I couldn't get comfortable just sitting outside on a bench either, no matter how beautiful the natural surroundings were while reading my books; for me it's necessary to have the comings and goings of a bustling coffee shop. So, for that change of pace I decided to see a place we passed on the way to church with Kate previously. I still have never been there, yet I sensed it had that warm inviting feel to it. Sort of like a Starbucks but whether they had more locations than one, I could not tell you.

I found a parking spot along the side in the far back and walked through the plaza glancing inside the stores along the way towards

Tropical City Coffee Roasters. Alexandria's liquors and wine. A neon sign reading Goose Island beers glowed in the window. An oversized bottle of Chopin Vodka resting on a shelf. Next door a carpet and rug sales room. Then after that was my destination, continuing to glance inward I saw a row of small tables with chairs, a few people sitting and chatting. A row of flavor syrups up high on the shelf and some seemingly artificial palm trees planted strategically throughout, hence the name of the establishment, Tropical City Coffee Roasters. I liked it quite a bit thus far especially being the coffee shop aficionado that I am. Then my heart sank immediately. Kate?? Was that her? Yes! Who was she with? It was a burly guy. He had a beard and reddish hair; I'd never seen him before, but they were sitting together at a table, however, off in the distance, so I had to take a closer look, but there's no way I could go inside. Too uncomfortable, I couldn't confront her now. I needed to observe what was happening. It wasn't good, no matter what her explanation would be. I had automatically made up my mind on that. I never considered myself a jealous guy, but I don't want my feelings hurt either. Focusing my attention, I pressed my hands to the glass and looked in-between them. She was smiling, now laughing. Damn! OK now she jokingly smacked him on the shoulder while still laughing. I paused a moment to think; then I walked along the same trajectory I was going, past the front entrance. A few more people sat in the arm chairs, a group of college aged girls maybe. Following the coffee shop was a bicycle store. My head clouded in confusion and maybe anger. Yes, anger, it is anger. I'm mad, but I want answers. I turned around and got in my car.

I suppose my change of pace didn't do me so good today but at least I know. I know *what* though? I know she is talking to someone else *and* I haven't heard from her in a while. I suppose I'd go back to Starbucks after all, although I wasn't in the mood. I wasn't in the mood for anything, but I didn't want to get back to my apartment either. So, I kept driving and when I got to a stop sign I looked in the rear-view mirror. Behind me I saw Larry from the Center. Could it be him, the founder, I had to say I was becoming increasingly more intrigued with him. Probably because he was a mystery to me. No, not just a mystery, many people are a mystery, but he, he was a successful mystery and I can see where Chen looked up to him like he was a role model. He had achieved what Chen wanted in life. Chen was stuck. He'd been able to get so far, and he's given the credit to Larry and the group, but he was on the verge of working full time for Larry and one step away from leaving the loathsome insurance company that he felt was holding him down. I could relate. And lately I'd felt that both Larry and Chen were also my ticket to some new scenery in life. If I stuck to them they could help me somehow. Maybe we could all work together and I could leave my hotel job. Maybe they needed my help to grow the Center? Could it be considered a "New Age" organization? And what would Kate think of all this? She'd made the clear statement to me on our first real date about her requirement, her boyfriend had to be a Christian. Yet she and I got along so well and were falling in love so quick. I felt it for some time now. But today I was sad.

I tried glancing back again to see if it was Larry; he'd been driving a Land Rover, an older model Discovery. I loved that type of car myself, but of course I couldn't afford one. I settled for a simple older model Honda Accord which got me from point A to point B. Keeping my eyes on the road ahead of me and periodically glancing behind me, I got really curious suddenly; where does Larry live? Does he have a beautiful house out here or does he live directly on temple grounds out in Litchfield county. If you can even call it a temple anyways. Then I remembered Chen's story about his wife getting undressed at the center. Oh wait, that was just a dream. I need a cold shower! Back to reality, I focused on the road. A car in front of me had a bumper sticker which read: '**NORMAL PEOPLE WORRY ME.**' At first, I thought, kind of ridiculous. But on second thought, someone like myself or Chen usually gravitated towards different kinds of people. And then there were really weird people who gravitated towards other *different* kind of people so in a sense they felt more comfortable with these kinds of people, hence normal people worried them. It reminded me of that song: 'It takes every kind of people.' OK so back to Larry. The Center was at least forty minutes away from us so what was he doing here. Chen lived somewhere in between where I was now, and the Center, hmmm. I pulled into the next plaza on my right when I got a chance and quickly turned around realizing the Land Rover drove onward. So naturally being as curious as I am, I decided to follow it. Yes, it would seem odd if I was caught following him but that wasn't what I was doing, was it? Ok yes it was, but I had to know more. What was I getting into after all? I don't want to get into a dangerous cult. Chen didn't seem dangerous and he didn't seem at risk; in fact, everything just seemed all too perfect with the group. Screw it, I was pissed about Kate being with that other guy. Just my luck she'd also claim I was following her or worse "stalking" all because I was in the wrong place at the wrong time. Or was it the right place at the right time? At least I was able to learn the truth. Up ahead Larry took a left. I didn't know this area; I didn't want to risk it any further. How awkward would this be after all if he saw me behind him, if he'd recognize me at all. Chen *did* give me that shout out in his speech. So, anyways, I made a mental note, Pine Road. I didn't know this area much after all. I'd just google it later. Maybe he'd lived there or maybe he just kept driving? Perhaps he was visiting his friends? I don't know.

I needed to blow off some steam. I'd worked out enough times lately. Quite frankly my body needed a rest. Plus, I didn't want to drive all the way to the Center. I'd go home to pray. Pray to God, the God of the Bible. There I'd find some answers; I'd have faith in that.

Chapter 17
Putting it All Together

As a philosopher, I learned a lot from Chen. I asked him so many questions. I took notes and of course in the back of my mind I'm leaving the possibility open to write a book of philosophical essays. Not the old dusty ones you read in philosophy class, but my own simple, plain-language view of life. Something anyone can pick up and read. Call it "Max's Modern-Day Philosophy," or something like that.

I learned that Chen was obsessed with his image, but not in the same way other people are. Not in the common egotistical way necessarily. With him it was more of a disorder that he had made great progress on but probably still has work to do. To him, it's important to exercise because exercise is therapeutic. It helps his mind and his body. Checking the scale to see if he's gone up in weight more than a couple pounds is a rule that he lives by. As for me, I can't go one week without completely reading at least one new book. As for Kate, she can't go a day without prayer. Also, it seems there are some sins she'll never commit. It's like some other people, to make the analogy, who just never get drunk. Maybe they'll have one or two drinks socially but for some reason unique to them, they don't cross that line. Others will never touch this drug or that drug. Some may have a phobia of sorts that prevents them from doing this or that.

Sometimes I wondered what Kate saw in me. I had to pinch myself to see if it was all real. She told me I was handsome every time we got together. And that I was very smart. Maybe it was God's answer to my prayer I made before taking my break from work. After all she's the Godliest woman I'd ever had come into my life. Perhaps that was just it, a blessing.

I'd learned about bullying through conversations with Chen. What really defines bullying? Years ago, he felt that it meant someone pushed you around physically, beat you up. When he was attending a lecture once, in his early twenties, the speaker asked, "Who's been bullied here in the audience at some point in their life." He looked around and several people raised their hands while Chen didn't. His experiences simply didn't fall in the category of bullying. So, he thought, anyways. Furthermore, he felt, by admitting to being bullied he'd be the weaker one and after all he hadn't been beaten up. Not only would he look like the weaker one compared to the bullies, but he'd look weak raising his hand in the room at the lecture. Let's face it, people all around us have problems but do they go around talking about them? Another way to put it: he hadn't really lost any fight. He'd been in a few shoving matches or some play fighting on the playground but so what did that mean? The topic of bullying had become so mainstream especially after events like Columbine or other shootings where the perpetrators had all been bullied in some way, shape, or form most likely. Chen got to thinking about the feelings of fear and day to day dread he'd been through during certain points of his youth. The reality that there was no known solution in sight on a day to day basis. Going to the principal or teacher would only cause the bullies to do him real harm, like even resorting to killing him. Was it reasonable to think so? He'd said one student who was a friend of the bullies but not part of the group of kids bullying him day to day happened to run into him in the hallway and threatened him with the words **"You're going to die"** if he'd show up at the local town fair that weekend. And this kid who threatened Chen's life was not all bark and no bite. He'd been seen pushing kids down the stairs from time to time. So much for safe Connecticut award winning public high schools. Clearly the other students in the classroom saw what was happening on a day to day basis and the teacher must have also. Although it was an art class in a gigantic room and the students were busy working on their projects, at some point and time things could have been handled. And why not right away? They could have put a stop to Chen's day to day torment. Perhaps those who step in and do something are heroes? The TV show "What Would You Do?" handled this topic beautifully. The hidden cameras would roll, and one actor would play the part of the victim and another would be the bully or person discriminating in some form for all to witness around the public space. Maybe a couple of actors playing the role of a black and white couple and a third actor sitting in the café playing the role of a racist. Would someone in the public stand up and say something? Would they intervene? Often emotions would run high and sometimes tears would come to the surface. The audience sitting at home resonates with it. In today's world where many live the life of boredom and stress at work then go home and feel a lack of any emotions at all, perhaps digging up real emotions is a part of the healing process. Maybe Chen had put all these feelings on the shelf years after they'd happened. He'd moved on and replaced those darker days with something different. But what? Do people resonate with a person shutting down and becoming quiet? No. Does putting up a thick armor of protection around yourself emotionally work to resonate with people? No. Often people turn to drugs and alcohol, food and other things to deal with a painful past or trauma in their life. And many in society say, "Stop drinking; you have a problem with drinking," but is drinking really the problem? So many are afraid to talk about what's underneath the surface. Secrets and lies start to form and little gets done to resolve anything. Maybe there's good reason why Chen and I have come together as friends. Maybe it's all interconnected? But Chen has done healthy things to overcome negatives from his past and he gives thanks to Larry. I'm intrigued with Larry and I'd like to know more by digging deeper.

We've all heard the common phrase: Everything happens for a reason. I think that it takes on a deeper meaning than a lot of people realize. It can mean what you want it to mean. For me, when I see that my life has gone the wrong way, rather than just say "why me?" and wonder, I can likely deduce a cause and effect which led me to my misfortune. Other times it's a mystery like in the book of Job from the Old Testament of the bible. Which reminds me of Kate once again. I can't stop thinking about her. She'd always had a strong Christian faith from the very beginning of her life. This included theology, structure in the household, and in the school. In her classroom growing up she'd learned a world view based on the Bible being taken quite literally. I on the other hand learned little in my studies as a Catholic. And in the public-school classroom I learned zilch on the topic of the Bible or creation science. Where did we all come from? How did the universe come to be? In public school you could never get the same explanation Kate got from her private education. But if what she learned was true, then what I learned in school was false. Two completely opposite viewpoints such as

evolution and creationism cannot both be true,
at least in my humble understanding. In fact,
they are completely different and at odds with
each other the deeper you dig into it. Didn't
measuring tree rings prove that the creation
science view point was wrong? I thought *this
way* not that long ago. But a short article I read
online gave me a counter argument which spoke
of certain weather conditions creating multiple
tree rings in shorter periods of time. Facts like
these opened me up to new study. Was it
possible for people to live as long as Adam of
the bible? Over 900 years old? It did start to
make sense to me once I read, yet again, more
counter arguments. The air early man breathed
was completely different. The environmental
factors were not what they are today. The ice
age was caused by Noah's flood. Soon enough I
realized there was a counter argument for every
single secular view point. Items so different
from each other such as broccoli, cinnamon, a
human being, a shark, all evolved out of
nothing? I didn't believe that. Next thing you
know, you start to realize how much the
television, newspaper, school and just about
every other facet of life in America revolves
around an evolutionary world view. I started to
see the words: 'millions of years ago' in so
many places. But how many people out there

are like I was, simply not hearing both sides of the story and thinking for themselves? *What a concept.* A lot more things in the Bible started to make sense such as the lineage of people leading up to Jesus. But how could so many Christian churches-of all the denominations out there-simply sweep these ideas under the rug. King David, sure he's part of the lineage, but what about Adam or those other names listed in between? Kate and I were in accord on these topics, which was exciting. The Larry Espenschied Center was all about honesty and speaking your truth. Would they be open to some of my thoughts? We'd see. Of course, after I'd seen her with that guy at the coffee shop, who knows what will happen between us next.

I started to realize that the Christian world view, although frustrating at times for me to fully accept because so many others rejected it, had solutions. Take for instance an aha moment I had recently at a new coffee shop I'd found. Many attractive women can be seen in towns like the one I was at that day. Older women who were fit and wore exercise clothing out and about. This one lady was in front of me in line and quite honestly, I was checking her out just for a second or two although she was much too old for me I most definitely found her attractive. But her conversation with the barista led me to my light bulb moment. She'd bragged about going to the Super bowl years ago because she was dating an executive who'd had such and such connection. She chatted sports teams and mentioned how good looking the man was, but "he was oh so boring" then she continued at a quieter tone of voice, telling the barista about something so superficial, about vanity, staying in shape, competing with other women who were younger etc. etc. and at that point I realized that this lady is very common among others I come across, particularly from certain areas in the state. But it just got me to realize that you have to put God first in your thoughts rather than base your life on a competition between yourself and the rest of the world. Who is more fit? Who has more money? Who is better looking? Those kinds of thoughts can lead you astray. And yet again Christianity can offer you an answer. But It's not always easy to swallow your pride and be humble. Maybe it'd get easier with practice?

Chapter 18

Time to Think. Night Drive

It was approaching evening and I'd felt cooped up in my tiny apartment for hours upon hours organizing, re-organizing, dusting, and reading. In a way, it felt pretty good, But the time came for me to get out of the house. Purposefully, I got in my car and did what I had always thought about doing for some time now-retracing my route to work and exploring the places along the way. The problem is I never went ahead with it because when I did get a night off from work each week I'd be already in bed sleeping or otherwise I'd feel like there was no point to getting out there, yet this time was different. When driving to work on the night shift you get to see civilization in the dark when things are a little quieter. Half the people are settled in for bed already and the rest are just settling down most likely. The lights might be on in a house or they might be off. Sure, some cars will still be in a hurry on the road, but it beats the morning rush. I'd adjusted quite easily to sleeping at night and being up during the day after a while on this "vacation" from work. So, I got in the car and just drove this evening. I'd gone by a local bar. Patrons walking outside for a smoke on the deck. I drove by much slower than usual to glance at all the goings-on. A neon sign read Budweiser. Another, Newcastle. I'd always told myself I'd stop in one day but never did. It was OK because I'd much rather go after making a change, job wise.

The life of the night shift worker is a strange one. Some will appreciate what you do with the common remark: "I don't know how you do it." It's always nice to hear that. Others will equate the day shift with the night shift as if there is no difference. "You're not used to the hours yet?" they'd say believing that you can ever really get used to them. Others will have some pity on you which actually feels pretty good especially when they say: "You're working till 7am?! God bless you! Or hang in there!" It's nice and surprising how just a few words can change the course of your life to some degree. Power of language I suppose.

The ideas kept swirling through my mind as I leaned back in my seat and coasted by, house after house, turning left, turning right. I saw a Dunkin Donuts up ahead and figured why not stop in. I got in line and they were a bit understaffed, so the line was long but the young lady behind me was looking at me; I just couldn't help but notice. Maybe she recognized me, but I didn't recognize her. We started a conversation and although I generally don't talk about work with everyone, I got on that topic with her for a minute and then I learned in fact she did know me. She'd stayed at my hotel on discount and worked at another property by the cinema off the highway, north of my hotel. All our hotels were more or less the same, so we'd be able to talk about many of the same things. Sort of like Dunkin Donuts, if you've been to one, you've been to them all! Nothing wrong with that, gotta love Dunkins. Well, that was like our brand hotel. We'd decided to sit down and chat after we got our coffees. I had my usual order, medium coffee with extra milk, no sugar. I offered to pay for hers but after pausing a moment to think about it, she insisted to pay for herself. I suppose it was more appropriate that way as I didn't want to turn this into a date, but I was glad to find someone awfully friendly to talk to and break up my night. Alejandra was her name and I'd never recalled seeing her before, but she'd named off people I worked with both currently and in the past, so I knew we'd have a thing or two to talk about. She'd excused herself for answering her cell phone and taking a brief pause in our conversation. She spoke Spanish rapidly to someone on the other end, but I couldn't tell what her ethnic background was. She seemed nice and was outgoing. I thought why not take this opportunity to vent a little about work and talk shop.

We sat and talked for almost an hour, so it seemed. I never got into anything that was on my mind as of lately regarding Kate or Chen, except for mentioning I had a girlfriend and I'd taken some time off work.

She said, "I want to move up in this business. I don't want to just stay where I am; I'm bored with that already. I worked in a full-service hotel and I got tired of that. I'm where I am now but I'm also in school. I'll either work my way up from supervisor to assistant manager to general manager, I don't know. Other times I wonder if I should leave this industry all together. I once got sort of burnt out at work. I knew management was in back shooting the breeze and I had a line up front. They could have come by, checked on me to see if I needed help. They have a damn camera on us after all. This kind of thing went on for a while. Once or twice the general manager walked right by casually even though he could see I needed a hand. I survived it, but it would have been nice to get some help. I started to wonder how valuable my work was to the operations of the hotel, so I started slacking off a little here and there. I started skipping some of my tasks daily just to see where It would lead. How much effect it'd have on the hotel."

She went on like this for a while. I got to thinking. I thought I had thought of it all before, but she was giving me new ideas. It's just that I'm the type of guy who'd feel guilty if I didn't do my required work. "I think working nights you have to sort of become a night shift warrior," I broke into the conversation again. "There are things I have noticed work and other approaches that just plain don't. I could write a book about it, put it online for sale like a real short e-book or something," I kidded. I have to give myself enough time at night. The more time you give yourself the happier you'll be on the way to work. It's just a personal preference but I prefer to take more backroads. Also, you need to plan out your night. Let's say you only give yourself forty-five minutes to get ready, well, you need to make that time work. Start your coffee maker when you first get up but don't wait for it to finish…"

"No?" she asked.

"No, because while it's brewing you're in the shower. You can weigh yourself on the scale, if you like to do that, when you first get up right before you jump in. After all you'll be naked at that precise time and on an empty stomach. When you're out and dried off, go grab your coffee. Use a mug that makes you feel good. Drink cold club soda but room temperature water. Sip orange juice; if you want to get fancy, pomegranate, guava or passionfruit, whatever. Mix it up sometimes and blend carrot juice with the orange. Be creative. Make sure you get enough sleep." I explained.

"Do you crash right after work and go to bed?" she asked.

"Almost never, you see, when you get home the sun is bright and you're awake. Sure, you can sleep then but you'll wake up in the early afternoon and be completely wired. You'll never be able to get back to sleep until well into the evening, and then, well then, you'll be doing a split routine with your sleep. That's OK but biologically I believe we're designed to sleep closer to night if not at night ideally! So just get into bed after one p.m. or so then get out of bed after nine p.m. or later.

"Wow, your whole day is kind of wasted then, isn't it?"

"Sounds a little depressing, *I know*," I responded.

"Does your girlfriend mind?" she asked.

"Kate, she's great but well let's just say I don't want to put her through any of this BS for too long. Maybe she's the inspiration I need to change. At least for now I'm on my one-month break from work. All of a sudden, I'm wondering if her and I are going to last anyways. You know what's weird?" I continued.

"No, what?" she asked.

"Well, you reminded me of when in the summer I did get into a routine just every so once in a while where I did nap in the morning and right around the middle of the day I was wide awake, and it'd offer me the perfect opportunity to go out there on the trail and jog like there was no tomorrow. It felt great. The sun beating down. I didn't care if it was one-hundred degrees because after I got into the car I just put on my music and took my water bottle, chugged it and it felt good. I felt like a million bucks. When I'd get home, I'd take a warm shower. I'd had a beer this one time after one of those mid-day jogs. They don't make it anymore. It's called Pete's Strawberry Blonde. I can still taste it on my tongue right now. I wonder why they stopped selling that beer? Oh well, and a little later my head hit the pillow. Then I'd have a couple solid hours to sleep. Sure, it's not much time but it was the deepest sleep ever. Then I'd get up feeling like a zombie, but I knew I was doing something good for my health with the exercise."

I glanced at my watch. She looked over at me. "Well I guess I'm going to have to head back," she said. I'm supposed to watch some movie with my friend. It's been nice talking to you. If I stay at your property again I'll stop by to say hi."

I went on my way and just kept driving. I wondered about Chen, I wondered about Kate, I thought about everything, but I felt pretty good strangely. I guess you could say I had some pretty strong mixed emotions. Things would work out though, I hope. I'm an optimist after all. And a conversation like I had tonight was just plain cool. A breath of fresh air.

Chapter 19

Going to the Top

At this point. I feel that all my thoughts and involvement of any kind with the Center are coming to a head. At the same time my relationship with Kate is at a rather uncomfortable point, which it has never been at before. My friendship with Chen is oddly also at an uncomfortable point, because he'd not been available when I tried to make plans with him. Maybe it was nothing, but I want to solidify my life a bit more and get some real answers. I'm starting to feel the way I did before I met either one of these two most important people in my life. Perhaps my mood was just in a weird place.

I have determined where Larry lives-with 99% certainty- through a google search which led me to a website on cults and groups. The people, leaving comments there on that website, had written about several different things. For example: how their girlfriends or boyfriends, family members, etc. had been involved with Larry's Center and had never been the same since. They'd divorced or broken up and so forth. One guy had paid "through the roof prices" for a one-week seminar back in 1999 in Atlantic City. Maybe they were just disgruntled or unenlightened to Larry's philosophy, but I was still on my mission to see for myself. And now I was a bona fide member. Well, on that website there were a couple of corroborating comments describing his street and house. Some landmarks and so forth but not an actual street number I could jot down. That's OK, I was fully intrigued beyond the point of no return and had to take a ride out there. Maybe I'm a little crazy, but I think the best course of action is to go directly to his front door. Every so often, during my life someone has said I was odd, strange, even bizarre. So why fit in and do everything according to the norm? What I *did* believe at this point was the old saying, made popular in the 90s: "WWJD? or What would Jesus Do?" Sure, maybe I was behind on the times, but pop culture in Christianity was just outside of my grasp back in those years, and after all, why couldn't this philosophy pertain nowadays? Some people, like a friar I met once, said "Jesus was a little crazy." This friar gave a talk at a church I visited out by Lake Ontario in Rochester, during my college days. But *I* don't like to put it that way. He, Jesus, was radical; I think we can all agree on that. One way or another I would need to feel His presence to confront Larry and get some clarity on everything with Chen, with the Center, with where I fit into all this and so forth. Maybe "confront" was the wrong way to think of it. "Confrontation" denotes hostility. Even the word "Encounter" can have a negative meaning if you look at the definition. Hmmm, if anything, the Center had done me good so far, but Kate must have had something against it. She was out with that damn guy! And, I just needed some answers during this fork in the road season of my life.

I got into my car and journeyed toward Larry's house. I didn't brew a coffee for the road   Because I just knew that he'd offer me a cup, that is if things worked out and he didn't just kick me to the curb or call the police. I felt a sense of determination as I turned the corner;

looking ahead I saw a green light turn to yellow so I just hit the gas and flew right through it. I heard a dog barking in the distance. It was unseasonably warm which felt nice. I didn't put any music on.

In life I recall a few memories where things were bothering me at least to some degree. Maybe it was a girl that I had a real crush on and it was driving me wild. I just had to make a resolution to the situation. So, in one case I finally got myself to drive out to the mall where she worked and ask her out while she was on the retail floor. Would you like to know how that ended? I'd rather forget. No, seriously it wasn't so bad because it was a small life lesson. She said she had a boyfriend, but if she didn't, she'd go out with me. To begin with, I found her attractive while I'd notice her at work. I'd worked at the same store with her but moved on to another place of employment by the time I went to ask her out. But back when I did work with her, I began dating another coworker and I was certainly no two-timer, so she'd be off my mind. I'd heard a rumor she'd said, "Why is Max with *her*, when he can have *me*?" Of course, this got my attention, but I wouldn't do anything about it. Then my co-worker girlfriend and I called it splits so suddenly this other girl at work was a real option. In the end, it was worth asking her out and it took guts. But at age nineteen I did crazy things like that. Another moment was when I had been troubled by a hotel transaction with a guest who would not provide a credit card for incidentals. There was already a credit card saved on file covering his room and tax according to the note on screen, so I didn't have to ask for one to cover that cost. He was part of a concert crew, which we tend to treat like royalty. His mood was terse, he acted rudely, and it was so late at night I just gave him his keys after checking his ID and he went his way after refusing to give me a card for incidentals claiming there'd be none. After all we had payment for the room and tax. Unfortunately, that payment on file was declined. Later that incident came back to haunt me as we needed payment and had trouble settling his bill. It got resolved for me personally when I talked it out, one-to-one, with my manager in his office. But up until that point it had bothered me. He'd said we need to talk on Monday, but he never showed on Monday and how much later can I stick around after being up all night at work. Then he said we'd talk on Friday and he never showed then either. Eventually when he finally did get to work on time to talk to me I got it over with. It's hard to

224

put into words, but these unresolved conflicts are going to change once you confront them. Whether the result is "bad" or "good" at least there is resolution. The girl turns you down? Well at least you know. The manager at work disciplines you? Well, at least you can ask questions and state your case, plus have a way to go forward if it happens again. With Larry, I knew that some kind of resolution would come to be after tonight.

So, while all these thoughts were swirling around my head, I just kept driving. I glanced down at the dashboard clock; ten minutes had passed. I was surprised when I learned his residence was less than twenty-five minutes from mine. Still, I was taking a chance not knowing for sure if he'd be home. What the hell was I doing? I started to break a sweat and my heart was beating a little faster than normal. I presume, about half his time he spends living at the Center in some mysterious room up high. Does he take one of the spiral staircases up? Does he take an elevator? Is there some other weird occult activity happening in some secret room? A room that mysteriously opens with secret commands, such as at The Magic Castle in California? Ultimately, I've been transformed over the course of these past few weeks. Soon I'd be returning to work and I'd have to decide about my life and how I'd go forward. It's like a powerful tug of war is going on secretly in my life: I've been affected so strongly by Larry, Chen, Kate and even other new people associated with them; I'm also so disgusted with my working life and truly at a fork in the road. Forty hours is a lot of time to devote of yourself to each week. Add the time it takes for you to get ready for work, plus driving and whatever overtime hours you put in. I rolled down the window a few inches to get some fresh air. Suddenly I'm getting closer to his house because I recognize the numbers descending on the right side of the road. I had read an estimate of street numbers but didn't know the exact one. I'm carefully looking out for Slippery Moss Road meanwhile the car behind me is getting impatient as my speed drops below 30 miles per hour. *Tough luck sir!* I think to myself. I'm going to have to be sure I don't miss this street. I turn right, he beeps the horn, looking in the rearview I see the driver's face contorted in an evil and angry expression while he throws his right hand in the air. Immediately he speeds around me. I drown out the thought of the irate driver, telling myself, I put my blinker on after all. Although I've never been up Slippery Moss Road, to me it appears as one of those roads which you are generally cautious on, because not only does it appear steep, but it also winds, and it's probably narrow, at least that's the view of it you have from the road below. We'll see. I climb upwards carefully piercing through the fog of this night, which has seemed to increase. I gently turn my steering wheel clockwise, as in fact the road does twist and turn. As I get higher, I glance down realizing my elevation. Vehicles below resemble matchbox cars at this point. I'm forced to make a turn now as the road splits. I come to a complete stop and take a deep breath, relieving my anxiety. It's beginning to look more like a state forest out here. I see a house to my right, but not another for a few acres, then again, several more acres. The pavement turns into gravel and I continue driving, glancing left and right. One land mark to look for is the sculpture of an oversized great blue heron in front of the house. Once again, I don't have a street number, but what I do have are descriptions I've read online. Let's hope what I read is in fact correct. The residence, I read, is a beautiful Tudor, Inspired by the homes in western Europe. The colors: white and brown. There's ivy all along the side. But while my mind wanders, my tires hit the dirt, and now, what was a reasonable gravel, has turned into bumpy earth, rocks, and twigs, causing me to realize that maybe I should have taken a right rather than a left back at that fork in the road. So, I turn around before I do any damage to my car and retrace my steps. When I do finally get on the right path, I realize the street name does in fact match what I read online. Just when I thought the road couldn't get any steeper I find what I'm looking for. After all, the other homes I'd seen didn't resemble the Tudor style. In fact, there are not many homes. Counting them, I discover there are five, and in the end, a cul-de-sac. But his residence is not at the end. It's second from the end. I park my car outside along the curb. The house at the end is slightly up at the apex of the neighborhood, giving them an overarching view of all the rest of Slippery Moss Road. It's a blue house with modern elements and strong angles. They turn on the light in the doorway clearly noticing me, even making eye contact. Suddenly they switch on a powerful flashlight and begin moving it in a sweeping motion across the yard. It's so incredibly quiet here that I can't hold it against them for being overly protective of their neighborhood.

Looking up, I glance into the night sky and its most definitely gotten darker since I've left home. I walk up the driveway which is on an incline and take the stone stairs up what had to be at least fifty steps winding slightly to the main entrance. His door is an ornate wood carved neatly with a smooth, clean finish. I use the lionhead door knocker rather than the doorbell. Looking back down the front yard towards my car, I spot the great blue heron statue next to a little pond, gazebo and bench. *Must be the place*, I think to myself.

His wife appears at the door. Mind you, I've never seen her before. Long, jet-black hair in curls resembles the radiant beauty of actress Andie MacDowell. I take a quick glance at her. Like Andie, she seems to be someone who truly looks attractive at any age. Well, I certainly hope that she is his wife, otherwise I came at the wrong time.

"Hello, can I help you?"

"Um yes, um I'm here to see Mr. Espenschied. Is he here?

"Let me check if he's available, now can I ask your name?"

"Yes of course. Sorry I didn't say so; I'm Max Kovacs. I'm involved with his center out in Warren."

"OK, Max, I'll be back in a moment."

Larry came bolting down the stairs and pulled the front door widely open signaling me to come in. I smiled back at him and asked, "Are you free for just a few minutes? I have something I'd like to talk with you about. I am a very close friend of your protégé Michael Chen, and I tried to reach you by email and could not get a response. I've had some things on my mind."

"Come on up," he said, walking me to the dining room area. I glanced to my left and saw an old Nordic Track piece of exercise equipment. "It's foggy tonight. I love the fog, don't you?" he asked.

"I love the mist and I love the fog," I responded.

Larry was good at breaking the ice. I think I'd discovered another reason I was drawn to this person. I'm a different kind of personality but so is he it seemed. Who else would talk about the fog like that? Most people just complain about fog, the rain etc., but I think you must be a certain kind of optimist to enjoy things like that.

"Rain is also nice; most people just complain about it," I added.

"It's nature's way of helping you get a sound sleep, among other things. Remember those little electronic gadgets, they would sell at The Sharper Image or Brookstone, which played the sounds of nature? You know? Crashing waves, the rainforest, the sounds of the loon, and so on. Well, you don't need them when you have the real thing," he said. But tonight, it wasn't rain, just a thick layer of fog in the air. The room was lit in a such a way that it was comfortable enough to see clearly but not bright. The lighting was quite remarkable the more I glanced around the room. Everything looked neat. Larry Espenschied himself was a neat looking person. I saw a gigantic colorful Rubik's Cube on the table. It had to be a sculpture purchased at some art gallery. His wife was even my type incidentally, looks wise at least, while I glanced off to my left, I saw her in the kitchen opening the fridge. I knew nothing about her. I suppose, in some weird way, the first five minutes of this unannounced visit was turning out to be worthwhile in general.

"Would you two like something to drink? We have a delicious emerald green tea from the tea shop at the mall I can make, or perhaps coffee?" his lovely wife asked. She had the refrigerator opened while she spoke to use. She was looking inside the fridge while leaning over. Wearing a long-sleeved shirt with narrow black and white stripes, the shirt fit her just right. When you look like that, you can pull off wearing anything.

"I'd like a cup of coffee please, milk and no sugar if possible, thank you," I said.

"I'd like the same, thank you honey. My wife Julie, Julie this is Max," Lawrence added with a smile.

"I want to talk to you about Chen," I said.

"Chen is a good guy. He's fascinating, really," said Larry. "And before I forget, the reason you didn't hear back from me, email wise, is because I've taken a short one-week break from those. I don't think we have to live as slaves to the email, and yes, I do have another account to handle my bills and other business, but we must remember to be human beings after all," he explained.

Ok that explained it, I thought to myself. "Chen's become my new best friend and in some of those exercises we were doing at your center, he's expressed a lot of concern about his working life lately. He feels he can come to live at your center and work with you as an employee. His living arrangements are not ideal, and he's had some bad experiences with his ex-girlfriend, financially leaving him stuck to live with his parents. But I feel he's really committed to what your cause is all about. Maybe you can help him out?" I said.

"Chen and I have been talking about this Max and he's going to be able to come live at the Center and work with me. He and I are going to put together a book on weight loss and he's going to be the co-author and he'll continue to do speeches. He's going to be really engaged at the Center, but I've been waiting for him to take the initiative and push a little harder for it. He only needs to ask, and I'd help him more."

"That's good Mr. Espenschied. There's more I'd like to talk about also…"

"Please call me Larry."

"OK, thank you… Larry, …. I'm feeling torn about something. Kate is a wonderful lady I've been dating. We've fallen for each other fast and things were going great up until recently. She's been understanding of my interest in your center, but now she's just questioning what place a serious Christian has at the Center. I mean for me, I don't see the conflict, and now I think she's gone off with someone else. All of a sudden, things are falling apart," I said.

Larry got up and turned, walking slowly towards a small table glancing out the bay window into the backyard. Picking up a blue, round glass sculpture with his left hand he twisted it in a circular motion, let it drop out of his hand while catching it in his right hand. He stopped to collect his thoughts, much like Sherlock Holmes would. He turned around towards me. "What I do is help people the way a psychologist would. I don't believe you can separate the spirit from anything you do, so my work deals in the realm of spirituality. You go to a counselor and they are afraid to talk about spirituality or God for fear of being politically incorrect. I've had this desire to just help people and base my work on the principles of honesty and expression of emotions or feelings. Am I a doctor? No. Do I have credentials in the field of psychology or counscling? No. My father was a medical doctor and he had money to begin with. When It came to my studies, he'd always stressed it was a must to go far academically. He helped get me into Dartmouth; he had connections. But the Ivy League was not a place for me. I left school midway through my sophomore year and branched off on my own. Ultimately, I had a passion for my work. I started working with people one-on-one and rented a space. I wrote a book. It was all coming together. People said I was brilliant and a great speaker to boot," he said.

I thought about what Larry was saying and glanced around the room. "That's a cool painting," as I pointed to a still life on the wall. Although Larry stopped to hear what I said he just continued his previous train of thought. Larry went on for a while speaking about his mission in life to help people and for the past thirty some years how he's been doing this and that and so on. All the while I got up and said I needed to stretch my legs if that was OK. Really it was only an excuse to look closer at the artwork on the wall.

Larry followed me by getting up and turning a dial off to his right which brightened the room. That's my daughter's work. Marigold, she's a graduate of Paier College of Art, here in Connecticut.

"Paier College of Art?"

"Yes, a small school, believe it or not, when she was attending, and she's probably around your age, there were less than three hundred students enrolled. Most people haven't heard of the school because it's so small but if they have heard of it, they usually have something positive to say about the very serious technical curriculum they offer in the arts. She, my daughter that is, studied fine art and got a degree over the course of four years. She lived in an apartment there on route ten, nice place. We helped her out financially. She really enjoyed her time there. She felt it was a different world entirely compared to the enormous public high school she attended. She wrote me this letter once. I'll never forget it. In the letter she talked about all the good times but also at one point having a feeling of being disconnected from the rest of the world. She said, 'dad, I'm so fixated on the world of art. Everywhere I go and everywhere I look I'm thinking like a painter, meanwhile most the rest of the people out there are working on computer programs and learning all this stuff, I'm just off in my own art world. It's not a bad thing but just something I've felt.' After college she was working in insurance, for a year or so, like our friend Chen. She switched jobs, moved around a couple times to different apartments. I was always there to pick up the tab financially if necessary. Then tragedy struck when my wife at the time, her mother, died. It was a car accident. She'd died instantly, and it came as a shock, of course, but my daughter took it the hardest. It's only her, so after the accident it was just her and I. It was hard on me too. I didn't meet Julie until a couple years later. I learned to move on with my life and I realized that things happen that are outside of our control. My life's work was to make sense of things and to help people, so I was able to help myself. My partner at the Center took over for me for a while but things were not right so we had to shut down more or less. I had money, so I guess work didn't really matter to me anymore. I'd had a friend Vincent who gave me the keys to his beautiful little condo, right on Lake Kenosia in Danbury. He would be out in Florida for six months, so I essentially just moved right in and used that time to find a "new me." I'd go down to the local coffee shop daily and drive up and down Mill Plain Road. Ironically nobody knew who I was at that coffee shop but that was OK. They got to know me, Larry, but not the semi-famous Lawrence Espenschied, author, self-help guru. I'd found a spa which offered wonderful massages that I'd schedule weekly. Ever since I've been a big supporter in the power of massage. The human touch was transformative for me. But through talking I helped Marigold, my daughter, with the loss of her mother. I was worried about her, she'd gone out late some nights into Hartford, New Haven, wherever there was a really happening bar scene. Was she partying with the wrong crowd? I don't know, but I knew it wasn't easy for her, and I talked her through everything, and she started to see the light again. She's my one and only biological kid, Julie has grown kids also from a previous marriage. That's where these paintings come from. These paintings are her creation after all of this happened. It was her idea to make a series. It had to be twelve she said. "Twelve paintings at least, no less, to make this particular series. Still life, nature paintings, up close portraiture, that type of thing. All in all, her best effort. I have half of them here. Beautiful colors, brushstrokes, all in oils. She gave this work everything she had. She started it here but finished the rest in Colorado. She said it was time for her to go. To pack up and move, start fresh. I was dating Julie then, as it happened. My daughter found love herself out in Colorado. She's engaged to a good guy named Tim. I went out there to meet him and hang out at her place. It all happened so fast. But its beautiful out there, Max. Her artwork is on exhibit full time at a top-notch gallery out in Colorado," he said.

I was thankful for Larry's story. He continued telling me how he'd given his daughter his blessing when it came to her wanting to marry Tim and in return she approved of her dad getting married once again. He spoke about how it was hard to get going once more after loss, and how in recent times Chen was like a catalyst for him to resurge. Chen's passion got Larry thinking of putting a book together with him and even considering Chen as a successor to the Center if Larry decides to retire.

"I think you should call your girlfriend Max; I know its bugging you," Larry said.

Kate and I had been playing this game of "let's see who will call first." Neither one of us had made that attempt to reach out, and days have gone by. I let Larry know my cell phone was left in the car, but he said it was not a problem and got up to reach for the house phone in the kitchen. I knew her number by memory and I had him dial it. I figured, if not now, when?

"Hello," she said. *God, I love her voice*, I thought to myself.

"Hi Kate, this is Max."

"Max, Hi, it's been a little while."

"Yes, I wanted to talk to you."

"I have been waiting for your call and was thinking you'd given up on us and moved on," she replied.

"No, it's not like that." Truthfully, I couldn't tell her that I'd seen her at that Tropical City Coffee place. How could I tell her that? I just so randomly happened to be at the same place at the same time as you and saw you there with another guy. I was scrambling for words to say when I knew it was now or never. "Listen Kate, I think we've had an amazing time together these past few weeks, but I don't think we should be dating other people. I just am looking for a one-on-one relationship," I explained to her.

"So am I Max. And what gives you the impression that I am seeing someone else?" She laid out the question as simple as that, which surprised me.

"I have reason to believe that you're seeing someone."

"And who? she asked.

"OK Kate, I didn't want to have to say this, but somebody I know has seen you out for coffee with another guy."

"WHERE?" She sounded angry.

"At Tropical City."

"What? Tropical City? When, who?"

"I hear that the guy had red hair, a beard and he was big, like he could play for the NFL. That's the description I got, OK? And I just don't want to play games with you here Kate. I need to move on with my life."

"Wait, wait, wait a minute. You're talking about my brother! That's my brother. Yes, now this is making sense. I was out with him at the Tropical City Coffee House or whatever it's called!"

"Your brother?!"

"Yes!"

Larry couldn't help but chuckle hearing our conversation, sitting next to me at the table.

"And my brother is protective of me. He is the one really questioning you, the Center, Chen, and all this stuff. He's looking out for me." Larry stood by rubbing his chin, thinking while he listened on. "Who is that laughing? She demanded I answer. "Is that Chen?"

"Can I speak with her Max?" Larry asked.

"Kate, OK um you know who that is? That is Lawrence Espenschied, he's here, well I'm here at *his* house. He's the owner of the Center and I came to talk with him one-on-one for the first time. And listen, he wants to speak with you. Is that OK?"

I handed the phone over. "Kate, hello, please call me Larry. I'm not going to keep you long, but I want you to know something important. Max loves you and I know this because I'm working very closely with Chen. Chen talks about Max. He talks about how he's madly in love with you and I feel it's important I let you know that there is nothing going on which should in any way get in between your relationship with Maxwell. I want to meet with you and I want Chen there and I want Max there and I want all of us to come together. We can make sense of all of this. I want to hear what you have to say, and I want everything to be in harmony. Larry went on like this speaking to her for another couple minutes. He explained how everything is interconnected and Chen hadn't been himself lately because he was upset over Max, Max is upset over Kate. It seems to be all a big misunderstanding. And now everything is resolving itself. I sat there and picked up my coffee which I had completely forgotten about and sipped it, savoring the flavor. While he talked I drank more and got halfway through the contents of the cup.

Maybe Larry needed us because it was his way of filling the void of his daughter who was not here or because of the loss of his first wife. Maybe it was just the continuation of the work he'd started thirty some odd years ago, which still wasn't finished. Maybe God was just blessing me with all these new people in my life to help me accomplish my calling. After he handed me back the phone, it turned out they'd already set plans for us all to meet tomorrow evening out at the Center, and yes Kate was looking forward to it. We'd make sense of everything; I just knew it. I can feel we all had respect for one another. Chen would be there at the same time because he'd already set up an appointment with Larry anyways, so if anything, seeing us there would be a pleasant surprise for Chen. Sitting here, in this dining room, on these soft cushioned chairs, glancing up at the skylight into the star filled sky, I felt my life was falling back into place.

"Do you like playing pool Max?"

"Sure, it's been a while…. a long while, but I'd like to."

"Come on downstairs and I'll show you my billiards room. Would you like another cup of coffee?"

"Sure, I'd like one"

"Next time scotch?"

"Yes, next time a little scotch would be great."

We walked down the stairs and he picked up his pool stick. This is Van Peusen.

"Is that a historical figure you've named your pool stick after?" I asked.

"No really just a fictional character."

"Well then, what happens if it's time to replace your pool stick? Like if it cracks or breaks," I asked.

"Then I shall call him Van Peusen the Second, Third, Fourth and so on. And, by the way, my wife would also like to join us for when we all meet tomorrow. She loves interesting conversations. She married *me* after all," Larry said.

I stopped to think for a second, smiling to myself. I didn't mind if Larry's wife joined us. No, not at all. Hey, I was just fortunate to have my own pretty lady joining us tomorrow. I turned my head to look around the room. He had a poster of ALF, the loveable, wise cracking alien from the 1980's TV show, framed up on the wall. "Beers of the World" read the next poster up on the wall, framed also. Hey that was the same poster from Luke's place that time. Maybe it was a sign. A "Peppers of the World" poster, Anaheim Red, Green Jalapeno, and so on with photos of different peppers. I guess he liked it hot. Nothing wrong with that. A Bose wave radio on the counter with a large hour glass next to it. A comfortable leather chair in the corner.

I realized, maybe I wasn't so odd after all; this guy named his pool stick after some bogus character. Then there was the ALF poster, and I hadn't even taken a tour of the house really. What would I find next? A statue of Max

Headroom? Plus, there was that "wild and wonderful" book I'd still yet not seen. And compared to Chen, well, Chen was at least as odd as me. And Kate, well, she is *dating me* after all. She can't be all that normal. What *is* normal after all? Why be normal? Be good, do good but be yourself. That's a good motto. Who would have predicted this strange turn of events? I've come to the decision that in a week's time, when I'm due to return to work, I'll go back to work, and I'll take it one day at a time. One week at a time and I'll decide from there whether I want to stay or whether I want to go. One thing is for sure; I won't last there forever. A Couple months, six months, maybe, one year, the most, then it's time for change. I got a text message earlier today, from a co-worker in management at the hotel, just expressing how they're looking forward to having me back and how much they really need me there to make the place run smoothly. It was nice, and it showed appreciation for what I do. I could only imagine the mess and clutter that accumulated without me there quite frankly.

In this moment, I got to thinking about the four of us: Larry, Chen, Kate, myself. In some way, we all needed each other. I have her to lean on. I have Chen to lean on as a friend.

We all must help each other out in life. Whatever happens tomorrow with us all will be like that "resolution of something which is bothering you" I spoke about earlier. Somehow things will be resolved when we all meet and talk it out. It feels like a paradox sometimes, to think God is in control. It's like a concept you must learn and realize in your life. But what could go wrong if I have *that* philosophy. Each has their free will. I can't convince Larry, Chen, my other friends, family and so on to think what I think. We can't make people practice or believe what *we* believe, but we can try to live a Godly life. I want God's will for my life. And yes, I am a Christian, and yes, that's the necessary foundation for my relationship with Kate. I know her family has expressed to her that they hope she'll get married soon, as she's getting older. It was too soon to get into it much with her, but now I know how badly I want to make that happen, so I'm going to do what I can to make her my wife. If it doesn't pan out, then there's a lesson in that. An experience, a memory. But Something inside of me says she'll say yes.

About the Author

Adam Kovynia is a first-generation American, born in 1981, in New Britain, Connecticut. He moved to Southington, Connecticut at age four and attended public schools and later graduated from Paier College of Art with a bachelor's degree in Illustration in 2003. He enjoys reading books at coffee shops throughout the nutmeg state, music and movies, especially of the 1980s and 90s, and sampling fine quality coffee, beer or rum. Some of his most memorable vacation experiences include anywhere in Florida, but especially Disney World, Poland, England, Vermont and the Creation Museum in Kentucky. He enjoys vegetarian cooking, massage, and learning new ways of understanding life. Adam is single and lives in Connecticut but thinks about moving to a new state in the not too distant future. *Max's Modern-Day Philosophy* is his first book.

CPSIA information can be obtained
at www.ICGtesting.com
Printed in the USA
BVHW09s0425100718
521026BV00006B/55/P

9 780692 142455